"You're mad!"

"I am what you made me," Vito responded very softly, a dark brilliance simmering like the start of a summer storm in the back of his fierce gaze. "The guy who gave you fabulous sex but no deep longing for a permanent commitment."

Ashley snatched up her abandoned coffee cup and threw it at him with an unrepeatable word. "How dare you talk to me like that?" she seethed.

The cup smashed harmlessly against the edge of the fireplace but the contents spattered Vito's jacket.

"If you want to behave like a wild animal, I will be more than happy to supply you with a cage."

D0822287

LYNNE GRAHAM was born in Northern Ireland and has been a fan of romance novels since her teens. She is very happily married with an understanding husband, who learned to cook when she started to write! Her three children keep her on her toes. She has a very large wolfhound, who knocks over everything with her tail, and an even more adored mongrel, who rules the household. When time allows, Lynne is a keen gardener and loves to cook Italian food.

Books by Lynne Graham

HARLEQUIN PRESENTS
1167—THE VERANCHETTI MARRIAGE
1313—AN ARABIAN COURTSHIP
1409—AN INSATIABLE PASSION
1489—A FIERY BAPTISM
1551—TEMPESTUOUS REUNION

Don't miss any of our special offers. Write to us at the following address for information on our newest releases.

Harlequin Reader Service
U.S.: 3010 Walden Ave., P.O. Box 1325, Buffalo, NY 14269
Canadian: P.O. Box 609, Fort Erie, Ont. L2A 5X3

LYNNE GRAHAM
A VENGEFUL PASSION

Harlequin Books

TORONTO • NEW YORK • LONDON
AMSTERDAM • PARIS • SYDNEY • HAMBURG
STOCKHOLM • ATHENS • TOKYO • MILAN
MADRID • WARSAW • BUDAPEST • AUCKLAND

ISBN 0-373-11696-1

A VENGEFUL PASSION

Printed in U.S.A.

CHAPTER ONE

ASHLEY couldn't sit still. She got up to pace her sister's kitchen again. Dear lord, how much longer would they be at the police station? Surely by now they realised that they had the wrong person? Her brother wasn't a car thief or a joyrider. He had respect for other people's property...hadn't he?

Tim was no angel—what teenager was? But he was intelligent. He had a promising academic future ahead of him. He would soon be sitting his final exams. Why would he go off the rails and attempt to steal a car? He had a car of his own, for goodness' sake!

Tim had been living here with her sister for the past two months. While their parents were in New Zealand, enjoying a long-anticipated reunion with relatives, there had been nowhere else for him to go. Unfortunately, Tim hadn't wanted to stay with Susan and Arnold. And Ashley had understood his reluctance. She wouldn't have wanted to live with Susan's rules and regulations either.

The white space-age kitchen reminded her of an operating theatre. It was sterile. There was no clutter— Susan would not allow clutter. Her home was obsessively clean and tidy. Just like Susan herself. On the phone, though, she'd been hysterical, or as close to hysterical as someone as repressed as Susan could get. Tim's arrest in full view of the neighbours had smashed her composure.

Break beyond the guidelines of Susan's rigid moral code and you were out in no man's land all on your own. A pariah. Nobody knew that better than Ashley. On the day Susan had discovered that her unmarried teenage sister was pregnant, Susan had turned her back without hesitation. When you threatened to become a

5

social embarrassment, Susan would literally cross the street to avoid you.

Ashley took sudden ironic strength from that awareness. If Susan had had the slightest suspicion that Tim might be guilty, she would have let Arnold go to the police station alone.

'Can I get you a cup of tea, Miss Forrester?'

Ashley spun round with a nervous jerk. Her sister's housekeeper, Mrs Adams, stood in the doorway, rotund in her sensible dressing-gown, her discomfort palpable.

'No, thanks. I couldn't,' Ashley muttered.

'Any word——?'

'Nothing yet.'

'He's such a . . . spirited young man,' the older woman remarked.

Ashley paled at the reminder. Tim had his father's temper. When he was roused, Tim was hot-headed and aggressive. Hunt Forrester rejoiced in Tim's ability to stand up to him. A boy was supposed to have grit and guts. A girl wasn't. Just as baby girls were the mistakes you had to accept on the road to fathering an all-important son, the second chapter in her father's book of sexist 'do's' and 'don't's' said that girls were supposed to be sugar and spice, rarely seen and never heard. Ashley had never fitted the rulebook. In one way or another she had always transgressed.

Ashley had rebelled but Susan had always conformed. Arnold had come along when Susan was eighteen. Although he was nearly twenty years older, he had been her sister's first and last boyfriend. Susan had never spread her wings in the outside world, never fought for a taste of the freedom which other young women took for granted. Ashley had often wondered if her sister had rushed into marriage to escape their domineering bully of a father and a home atmosphere riven with tension and frequent angry scenes.

'That's the car. . .' Mrs Adams tensed. 'I'll go back to my room, Miss Forrester.'

Ashley pushed a nervous hand through her dishevelled mane of red-gold curling hair and took a deep, steadying breath. Susan didn't know she was here waiting and her sister would probably see her presence as an act of unwelcome interference. As she heard the key in the front door, she walked out to the hall, praying that Tim would walk in, angry and shaken but unafraid...in other words, an innocent accused. Dear God, she couldn't even bring herself to consider the alternative!

The lanky youth who lunged through the door at full tilt didn't even see her standing there. Tim raced upstairs and the loud slam of a door ricocheted through the house. Arnold appeared next. In the act of shedding his raincoat, the older man froze. 'Ashley?'

Susan thrust past him. Her oval face was a waxen mask, stamped by bruised eyes and two burning spots of enraged red. 'Ashley?' she exclaimed shrilly.

'Susan——' Arnold planted a restraining hand on his wife's sleeve.

'Stay out of this!' Susan rounded on her husband furiously. 'She's here and I'm glad she is. I *want* her to know what she's done!'

'What *I've* done?' Ashley echoed after an incredulous pause.

'This is all your fault!' Susan hissed at her. 'What am I supposed to tell Mum and Dad when they come home? They put Tim in our care. He was our responsibility. When Dad finds out about this, he'll blame me for ever letting you near Tim. You don't need to worry! Dad won't come calling on you for his pound of flesh!'

Susan in a rage was a stranger to Ashley. She had the weird feeling that she had stepped into a crazy mirror-world where familiar people become unrecognisable. As a rule her sister was frigidly unemotional, but tonight she was a woman possessed, alien in her spitting belligerence.

Ashley moved a pleading hand. 'Susan, please. I don't know what you're talking about. How can I be involved in this?'

'Aren't you involved in everything that drags our family down? Do you know whose car he wrecked?' Susan ranted. 'Do you know why he wrecked it?'

Ashley was in a daze, devastated by the obvious admission that Tim was apparently guilty as charged.

'Our stupid little brother went out to get his revenge on the man who left you in the lurch four years ago!' Susan's enraged face suddenly crumpled and she half covered her wobbling mouth with her splayed fingers, denying the tears that were threatening. 'So what does he do? He takes his car and goes beserk with it in the grounds of his home! He's caused thousands and thousands of pounds' worth of damage. That car cost more than this house did! And it's a write-off!' Her shaking voice was rising steeply. 'He's demolished their b-bl-blasted stupid fountain and ripped up their bowling-green lawn! And for that, he's likely to go to prison!'

'But that's impossible,' Ashley whispered through bone-dry lips.

As Arnold attempted to comfort his wife, he was elbowed rudely away. Her sister fled upstairs as Tim had done minutes earlier. In the earth-shattering silence that she left behind, another door slammed.

'She can't bear to have anyone see her cry,' Arnold sighed, steering Ashley into the lounge. 'Best leave her to herself until she calms down.'

A wave of dizziness was assailing Ashley. White as a sheet, she swayed and braced herself with both hands on the back of the sofa. It was impossible. It couldn't be true. Tim didn't even know *who* she had been involved with while she was at university. Somehow Susan had got hold of the wrong end of the stick, lost her head and made quite insane accusations.

Over by the drinks cabinet, Arnold was talking to himself. 'None of us is to blame. The boy's out of control, but he was out of control long before he came to us.'

'Tim couldn't possibly have taken...Vito's car,' Ashley said unsteadily.

Arnold sipped at his whisky. He had forgotten to offer her a drink. That oversight spoke volumes for his state of mind. 'I'm sorry, my dear. You're still in the dark, aren't you? Take it from me, you'd be wiser staying there,' he completed heavily.

'Arnold!' Ashley wanted to scream and shake him out of his lethargy. 'I need to know what's going on!'

Her brother-in-law took a deep breath. 'Tim goes to school with—er...Cavalieri's nephew, Pietro.'

'He never told me that!' Ashley burst out.

'Until recently, Tim had no idea that there had ever been any previous connection between our family and the Cavalieri clan.' Lines of strain were grooved into Arnold's thin features. 'At one stage, believe it or not, the two boys were actually firm friends. Pietro moved with a fast crowd and Tim was popular with them. It was Pietro who started up that trouble at that nightclub, but, since his family have more influence than we have, poor Tim carried the can alone——'

'What trouble?' Ashley interrupted blankly.

Arnold groaned. 'He was up before the magistrates in the spring for disorderly conduct and criminal damage after getting into a fight.'

Ashley closed her stricken eyes. 'Does nobody tell me anything?'

'To be fair, he got in with the wrong crowd.' Arnold sighed. 'And after that nightclub business he did realise that he'd been handpicked as the fall guy. The club had no intention of pursuing a Cavalieri to court.'

'So this wasn't Tim's first offence,' Ashley registered in horror.

'The friendship with Pietro cooled after that, but last month Tim attended a party at Pietro's home,' Arnold continued with visible reluctance. 'Someone there identified him as your brother. The two boys had already been involved in some silly rivalry over a girl. Pietro jumped on the bandwagon, made certain offensive remarks concerning—er—your past—er—relationship with his uncle, and there was a fight.'

Ashley's knees gave. She felt her passage down into the nearest seat, her stomach knotting up with nauseous cramps. Arnold managed to avoid her anguished stare.

'Tim thumped hell out of the little swine and he was thrown out,' he said grimly. 'But unfortunately, Pietro wasn't prepared to take his come-uppance lying down. He and his friends, having found Tim's weak spot, continued to bait him at school. And last month, four of them cornered him and beat him up.'

An inarticulate gasp of distress escaped her bloodless lips. She remembered how uncommunicative Tim had been about that episode. She had got nowhere when she tried to find out what had lain behind that attack. Tim had stared at the wall. He had almost stormed out when she'd persisted. In the end, she had minded her own business. She had been the black sheep of her family for over four years and her only recently renewed link with Tim had been too tenuous and too precious to risk.

She bent her head sickly. 'Go on.'

'Susan and I were extremely disturbed when he refused to tell us what had provoked that attack. We did think about approaching the school but I felt that Tim would find that humiliating. I expected it all to blow over. Believe me, I regret that decision now.'

'But why didn't he tell us what was happening?' Ashley moved her head in a numb motion, too shaken to think straight.

'You have to view this situation and the players involved without rose-tinted specs,' Arnold said flatly. 'I'm afraid I've never had much time for your father's determination to exclude you from the family circle. It's caused enormous stress to everyone concerned, particularly to your mother and Tim...'

The carpet blurred beneath Ashley's swimming eyes.

'Tim's very attached to you and very loyal. He didn't trust us enough to tell us what was happening.' Arnold hesitated. 'And, much as I love my wife, I find it ridiculous that after twelve years of marriage Susan is still so desperate to win her father's approval that she is willing to cut her only sister out of her life just because he demands that she do so.'

It was coals of fire on Ashley's head. Susan had scars from their childhood as well. She simply dealt with them differently. Ashley tasted blood in her mouth. Involuntarily she had bitten her tongue. 'I'm sorry,' she whispered.

'You have nothing to apologise for. Tim went out to level a personal score,' Arnold asserted. 'He broke into the grounds of the Cavalieri home, started the car, couldn't control it and left a trail of destruction behind him. He ran off before he could be caught but he had been seen.'

Ashley was feeling physically ill. Her past had obtruded painfully into Tim's present. In her name, he had been provoked, humiliated and driven into an attempt to strike back. 'Has he been charged?'

'Of course. The Cavalieris own one of the biggest banking concerns in Europe. Tim won't talk his way out of this little lot. But he's brought it on himself.'

'How can you say that?' Shaking briefly free of her shock, Ashley leapt upright. 'He defended me and now he's paying for it!' Tears streaked her cheeks.

'Vandalising someone else's property is hardly in line with a gallant defence of one's sister.'

'How else could he hit back?' Ashley gasped. 'I know he's acted like a great overgrown child but Vito's family are so filthy-rich and powerful, he couldn't have touched them in any other way!'

A dismayed furrow divided Arnold's brows. He didn't like the direction the dialogue was taking. 'We'll get him the best legal representation we can afford,' he replied stiffly. 'But it ought to be your father in the dock. Tim should have been disciplined long ago.'

'I'll go up and see him.' Ashley had no time for his fastidious platitudes. They were not going to help Tim now.

Tim was sitting at the foot of the bed, his hands clasped white-knuckled between his thighs, his untidy auburn head bent. He didn't look up. 'I didn't know you were here until I heard your voice downstairs.'

'Arnold's told me everything.' She leaned back weakly against the door. 'Why, Tim? Why? Vito never did anything to you...'

His head flew up. 'Oh, no? What about you?' he demanded bitterly. 'He wrecked your life. You had to drop out of uni. You're not allowed in your own home. You live in a lousy bedsit, work in a lousy, demeaning job because of him!'

Her brother's bitterness pierced her flesh like so many knives.

'And that foul-mouthed little creep Pietro sneers about you like his uncle did something to be proud of!'

'You don't know what happened between Vito and me,' she said haltingly.

'You were nineteen and he was twenty-eight,' Tim flared. 'That tells me all I need to know.'

'Our relationship just didn't work out, Tim.'

'He dumped you when you were pregnant and married someone else,' Tim snapped back rawly.

She was drenched in pain by the blunt reminder of the child she had eventually lost. Grey-faced, she whispered tightly, 'It wasn't like that, Tim. He didn't know I was pregnant. In fact, at the time we broke up, neither did I, and I never told him. There wasn't much point once he was married.'

Her brother stared at her incredulously. 'Don't lie about it! I'm not a kid any more.'

'But that's how it happened.'

His complexion had a sickly hue now. 'I don't believe you. He let you down. He left you in the lurch. He used you! He must have known about the baby! He must have...'

'Does Pietro?'

'Well, no, but——'

'Vito didn't know.' Her nails had bitten sharp crescents into her palms. Too late now to wish she had told him the whole story. But how could she have told him so that he would have understood? Some things you didn't want to talk about. Some things you couldn't explain to a teenage boy, who was determined to see his much maligned sister in the guise of an innocent victim, seduced and abandoned. In one sense, it had been that brutal, but in another sense she had chosen her own fate. And Tim's response to her questions had confirmed her every suspicion. What had driven Tim over the edge was her situation, not his own.

'Try not to worry too much,' she murmured. 'It may... it may just come all right.'

'I'm not a baby, Ash,' he muttered jerkily. 'I fouled up. In the pub, it was all just spinning round and round in my head. What they'd done to you. What they'd done to me. I just couldn't take any more. I just... I just saw red, you know?'

Yes, she knew exactly. In temperament, she and Tim were very alike. They had their father's quick, seething temper and it was a curse. A curse and a weakness she abhorred.

Arnold was waiting downstairs for her. 'I'll drive you home.'

'No, really... there's no need.'

He draped her jacket round her slumped shoulders. 'Come on. I need some fresh air.'

She had to give him directions. Apart from one enquiry as to how she was getting on with the Open University degree she was studying for, there was no further conversation. Both of them were buried in their own thoughts. But Ashley felt that she had the advantage.

After all, she knew what she had to do. She had to see Vito. He had at least to give her a hearing. And if she had to crawl, well, she would do it. If that was what it would take, so be it. Ashley and her pride were an inseparable duo but, where Tim's freedom and her mother's peace of mind were concerned, no sacrifice would be too great. It would be her penance for what Tim had had to suffer in her name.

As she slid tiredly into bed, the paralysis of shock was seeping away. The full horror of the night's revelations was sinking in. Oh, dear heaven, why had this had to happen? How many times did she have to pay for one mistake, a mistake that, given her background, should have been easily avoidable? The mistake had been falling blindly, hopelessly in love with the wrong person.

Her mother had made the same mistake after all. Sylvia Forrester didn't have a strong personality, however. Quiet and gentle, her mother would always follow where others led. After thirty-odd years of her husband's bullying, she was an apologetic, self-effacing woman, far too weak to cross a man who had made a proud god of masculine domination. She had already had one nervous breakdown.

At eighteen, Ashley had been supremely confident of her ability to control her own emotions. She had had her entire future mapped out like a battle plan before her. University, a top-flight degree followed by a meteoric rise to prominence in the business world. Instead she had plummeted like a stone in the first year of her course. Why?

For a crazy five-month span she had lost sight of her goals. She had forgotten the lessons ground into her by her own upbringing. And, to make it even worse, she had honestly believed that she knew what she was doing. It was wonderful the excuses you could make to yourself when you wanted something you knew you shouldn't have. And that put her feelings for Vito then into a nutshell.

Something forbidden, something dangerous, something out of control. Once she had prided herself on her self-discipline. There had been no place for a man in her battle-plan. Men took, men demanded, men expected, men complicated things. Maybe when she was at least thirty, she had thought with the naïve certainty of youth, maybe when she was comfortably established in her career, she would let a man into one compartment of her busy, fulfilling existence. 'He' would be enthusiastically supportive of her ambition, content to accept that only that one tiny little compartment was his...

Fate had had the last laugh on her. Fate had thrown up Vito, a male as diametrically opposed to her ideal as he could possibly be. Once Vito had believed that he had her where he wanted her, so besotted she couldn't think straight, he had tried to change her into a totally different person. Piece by piece he had eroded her confidence, criticising this, censuring that. Thank God she had woken up.

One day she might have looked in the mirror and seen her mother staring back at her. An unhappy woman, hooked on a man who was poison for her but too drained of strength and self-worth to take the antidote. It would be news to her sister, but in Ashley's opinion there could have been no worse fate than to end up respectably married to Vito di Cavalieri...

'There is no point in waiting any longer.' The receptionist flashed her an irritated look. The phase of meaninglessly polite smiles was long past. 'I did warn you that Mr di Cavalieri wouldn't be available. When he's in London, he's exceptionally busy. His appointment book is filled weeks in advance.'

He wasn't available on the phone and he was no more available in the flesh. He *had* to see her. He simply had to. He knew why she was here and he had to understand. There was nobody more family-orientated than Vito. She had called in sick at the day nursery where she worked as an assistant. On the dot of opening time, she had entered the Cavalieri Bank. Two hours on, she was still on the ground floor of a twenty-storey building. Perhaps it was naïve of her, but she was appalled by the growing suspicion that Vito wouldn't even give her five minutes of his time.

Her surroundings reeked of expense and elegance. Cross a brain like a steel trap with the family bank vaults and you got success, the sort of success that even the receptionist wore like a mantle of superiority. Ashley reddened, painfully conscious that four years ago she would have strolled into this impressive building in jeans and a T-shirt and an unconcerned smile.

Then, it wouldn't have bothered her that she looked shabby and out of place. In those days she had been secure in herself. But she wasn't now. As the axe of retribution had fallen on every hope, dream and attachment she had ever cherished, her self-confidence had dive-bombed accordingly.

Vito wasn't going to see her. She tasted the concept, retreated from it fearfully. All right, so they hadn't parted friends. In fact, they had parted on the most violent terms of mutual hatred, but somehow she had assumed that Vito would opt for the civilised response.

'Miss Forrester?' It was the receptionist again. 'If you're prepared to wait for another hour, Mr di Cavalieri may be able to see you. It's not definite now,' she warned. 'His senior secretary is trying to squeeze you in before lunch.'

Ironically, that condescension sent fury hurtling through Ashley. 'How very kind of her,' she said sharply.

'You can wait on the top floor,' she was told frigidly.

The top floor was sumptuous. Involuntarily she was impressed, and that annoyed her again. The svelte brunette on the desk looked her over covertly. The loose khaki jacket and cotton trousers she wore were the closest thing she had to a suit. Her hair was doing its usual stint of falling down, dropping untidy tendrils round a face that already felt horribly hot. In all, she felt a mess.

By the end of another hour, she was a limp rag. All her carefully thought out opening speeches and follow-ups had deserted her. Vito, she was convinced, was deliberately keeping her waiting. Vito had the art of subtle, mindbending cruelty at his polished fingertips.

'Mr di Cavalieri will see you now.'

Gulping, she scrambled upright, hating him for having reduced her to a bag of nerves, harassed by unwelcome memories. A middle-aged woman greeted her at the foot of the corridor. 'I'm afraid Mr di Cavalieri can only give you ten minutes.'

Ten minutes to plead Tim's case to a male who not only loathed her but also equated dropping a sweetie paper on the pavement with crime? She hung on to a hysterical howl of laughter. Ten minutes was better than nothing and, knowing Vito's capacity for holding on to a grudge, nothing was what she had almost received.

Double doors spread wide into an enormous office. An acre of plush carpet stretched before her. She could see a desk with a computer bank and several phones. Psychologically, it was a most intimidating backdrop, reminding her quite unnecessarily that she was entirely on Vito's ground with nothing between her and desperation but the flimsy hope that he did not recall their last meeting quite as accurately as she did...

Her skin dampened. Vito was in view now. Taller than she remembered, darker than she remembered, about a hundred times more staggeringly attractive than she had ever allowed herself to remember. All the sophisticated trappings were there: the superbly elegant suit, the absolutely unshakeable good manners that were prompting that coldly polite smile. But they were only a façade on a fiercely elemental nature and an immense and arrogant ego, a galaxy away from her New-Age-man ideal.

'Thanks for seeing me.' It wasn't the opening she had planned. Indeed, it sounded demeaningly humble to her own ears.

CHAPTER TWO

'I'M SURE you'll understand that I'm not being rude when I ask you to be brief.'

Vito indicated the chair placed in readiness about six feet from the desk. If his secretary had stepped forward with a blindfold, Ashley wouldn't have been surprised. 'I'll be as brief as possible.'

A satiric black brow elevated. 'Bearing in mind that I have no desire to hear a plea for clemency on your brother's behalf.'

Crushed before she could even warm up, Ashley was relieved when a phone buzzed and he stretched out an impatient hand. As his attention switched from her, she breathed again. The temptation to study him was overpowering. He was incredibly attractive. Hard cheekbones slashed his strong, dark features, highlighting the proud temperamental flare of his nose and a mouth that was a wide, blatantly sensual arc. But, if you were a woman, it was the eyes you noticed first and remembered longest. Vito had stunningly beautiful eyes, golden as the purest precious metal in sunlight or dark as darkest ebony.

In defiance of her every wish to the contrary, Vito still radiated a dark, savage sexuality boldly at variance with a three-piece suit and a silk tie. Every woman between fifteen and fifty raised her chin and sucked in her stomach when Vito passed. And she was not, she learnt, dragging her disobedient eyes from him, the exception that broke the rule.

As she lowered her lashes, her skin heated. A tiny pulse at the base of her throat was racing. She was badly shaken by her adolescent response to all that raw, blatant masculinity. Anger followed predictably in the wake of that lowering awareness. He replaced the phone, uttering a bland apology for the interruption.

'You want me to get down on my knees and beg, don't you?' As the hot, thoughtless words burst from her, shrill with resentment, she could have bitten her tongue out for that loss of control.

Vito lounged back in his swivel chair, insultingly unsurprised by the verbal assault. Far too perceptive eyes of gold ran over her flushed face. 'Exactly why are you here?' he asked, politely ignoring her outburst.

'To talk about Tim and why he did it. You're probably not aware of it, but your nephew——'

Vito dealt her a narrowed glance. 'Insulted you to your brother?' he interposed. 'It was a regrettable incident.'

Ashley stiffened. 'Regrettable?'

'Pietro lost two of his front teeth,' Vito returned drily. 'The question of family loyalties was settled with their fists. Pietro came off worst and he has been honest with me. I see no connection between that episode and your brother's inexcusable invasion of my home.'

'So you had chapter and verse on Act One. What about Act Two?' Ashley pressed with spirit. 'Tim was cornered outside school and beaten up by four boys, one of whom was your nephew.'

'When did this take place?'

Ashley had to think for a second or two before slinging the date at him with relish.

'On that day, Pietro was attending his cousin's wedding in Rome,' Vito responded even more drily. 'He could not possibly have been present.'

Her chin came up. 'If he wasn't there, he organised it.'

Vito set the gold pen in his hand very decisively down on the glass desktop. 'You are now entering the realms of fantasy. Pietro would not have involved himself in so cowardly an act. Unless you have evidence on which to base these allegations, I would advise you to drop this line of argument.' Ice cool dark eyes rested on her.

'Pursue it and you will find it a most unproductive course.'

She was furious that she did not possess the exact details of that incident. Four youths had attacked Tim. That was the sum total of her knowledge. She ground her teeth together on an explosive retort. The atmosphere had all the encouraging warmth of a polar freeze. Biting her lower lip, she murmured, 'I understand that the enmity between your nephew and my brother originally related to some rivalry over a girl——'

His sculpted bone-structure set. 'And what possible relevance does that information have to the current situation?'

Ashley stiffened. 'The connection is pretty obvious from where I'm sitting!'

'Then we would appear to be seated in very different positions,' Vito drawled with biting sarcasm. 'I fail to see the smallest connection.'

'You're not prepared to allow me anything, are you?' she snapped back at him, her temper simmering.

A chilling smile formed on his lips. 'But then, in your place, I would have come through that door and endeavoured to make what apology I could for such conduct. Your sole reason for being here appears to be a blind determination to foist some measure of blame upon Pietro or, indeed, upon some unknown girl,' he delineated with sardonic emphasis. 'If that were not so contemptible, I would be entertained by your efforts to excuse the inexcusable.'

A red-hot flush climbed with painful slowness beneath her translucent skin. Her approach had been all wrong. She didn't need *him* to tell her that. Vito, hatefully polished veteran of many a brilliant diplomatic manoeuvre. Just entering this office had taken every shred of courage in her armoury. Under threat, Ashley went on the offensive. If Vito had been decent enough to see her earlier, she could have controlled that flaw in her own make-up. But Vito had made her suffer through an agonising morning of uncertainty, adding to her stress and strain. Vito had successfully smashed her composure before she even walked into this room.

'I was...I *am* very upset,' Ashley reasoned tautly. 'Tim's been under considerable pressure recently with his exams so close. I simply wanted you to have a clearer picture of his state of mind.'

'But I have not the remotest interest in his state of mind,' Vito said without a flicker of emotion. 'He is neither a child nor a mental incompetent. He is responsible for his own actions.'

She focused on a point safely to the left of him. This was it. This was her cue to explain why Tim had reacted so violently to Pietro's taunts. This was her cue to tell Vito that their relationship had, in the messy aftermath of their break-up, extracted a heavy toll from her future. But how could she possibly manage to tell Vito about her pregnancy? Vito, of all people? How on earth could she discuss something that was so deeply personal a grief that she had never yet managed to discuss it with anyone?

In a weak moment she had allowed Susan to know that she was carrying Vito's child. She had trusted Susan to be careful with that information. She should have known better. Her father had overheard Susan and Arnold talking about her pregnancy and the secret had been out with a vengeance!

Hunt Forrester had always been the first to sneer when other people's children got into trouble. He would boast of the rigid discipline within his own home, censuring other more liberal parents and smirking over the unlikelihood of any of his children making the same mistakes.

The discovery that she was pregnant had outraged her father. The fear of his own loss of face in the local business community, should her condition become known, had been enough to make him disown her. The further news that the father of her child was already married to someone else had been the last straw.

She had been four months pregnant when she'd miscarried, although most of her family had assumed that the loss of her baby was not a natural event. She had been hoist with her own petard. In her teens she had been very outspoken about her determination never to marry or have children. Everyone knew that abortions were relatively easily available and everyone had assumed that she had finally chosen that option. No, she could not tell Vito...Vito, who was so exceptionally fond of children, Vito, with whom she had once enjoyed several heated debates on the subject of a woman's right to choose. Vito would not believe her either and, if he thought for one moment that she had chosen that option, he would despise her even more than he did now.

'Tim is only eighteen,' she started afresh, ramming back the bitter pain of her memories. 'And some of this is my fault. I never discussed...I mean, he knows nothing about what happened between us. He made certain incorrect assumptions but I had no idea how he felt until this happened...'

The silence dragged on. Vito could use silence like a weapon. She had never been able to understand how he achieved that effect but he did. He sat there, supremely at ease, cool, calm and immensely self-assured. He intimidated her. Her slender hands clenched even more tightly round the bag on her lap. 'Look, I'm not trying to excuse him——'

'But that is precisely what you are guilty of,' he countered.

The word 'guilt' sent spectral fingers of alarm wandering down her rigid spinal cord. 'If Tim receives a prison sentence, his whole life will be destroyed. He lost his head, Vito. He's very sorry for what he's done.'

His gaze was unwaveringly direct. 'Then where is he?'

'He doesn't know that I'm here.' She floundered wildly for a second. 'And I don't know why you're even asking me that. It's unfair. You've stirred up the police so much, he'd probably be arrested if he came anywhere near this building!'

'Agile,' Vito murmured softly, appreciatively. 'I had forgotten how agile you could be. But tell me, if either

I or any member of my family had been in the path of
that car, do you think your charming brother would have
stepped on the brakes?'

Bone-white, she flinched. 'Why do you want to make
what he did even worse than it already is? He ran amok
with your car. He didn't try to kill somebody! It was
done on impulse while he was under the influence of
alcohol. He didn't know what he was doing until it was
too late!'

Vito made a flexible bridge of long brown fingers. 'Is
that alarming assurance intended to soften my heart?
Those who break the law should be punished.
Cushioning your brother from the consequences of his
own behaviour would not be in his best interests.'

'It was only your blasted car, Vito!' she slashed back
at him furiously. 'He didn't plan to crash it. There's
punishment and punishment. Sending a teenager to
prison for smashing up a car and a stupid fountain is
what I call over-reaction. It will destroy Tim!'

'It's most unlikely that he'll go to prison for a first
offence.'

'But it's not his first——' In horror, she caught back
what remained of that killing sentence.

Black lashes dropped reflectively low on brilliant dark
eyes. 'My conscience may then rest in peace. Quite deliberately you have sought to mislead me by contending
that his behaviour was quite out of character. But if he
has broken the law before, he most definitely deserves
what he has coming to him. Clearly the first warning
was insufficient to curb his violent tendencies.'

A steel band of tension was now throbbing across her
brow. She had come here to help Tim. So far, all she
had done was fuel the flames of Vito's outrage. 'Have
you ever met Tim?'

'Very briefly,' Vito conceded. 'I recognised him at my
nephew's party and had a short conversation with him.
He bears a marked resemblance to you in both colouring
and temperament.'

'Do you think I have violent tendencies as well?' she demanded bitterly as she realised that Vito, probably quite unwittingly, had been responsible for connecting her brother with her for the benefit of the rest of his family.

He ignored the gibe. 'He has your eyes,' he said very quietly, his sensual mouth hardening. 'You both possess considerable physical appeal but in his case, as in yours, it is distinctly superficial on closer acquaintance.'

Temper stormed through her and she lifted her head high. 'You do have to concede one mitigating factor, however...'

He sighed, glancing fleetingly at his watch, boredom somehow screaming from the tiny gesture, making her even more determined to explode him out of his offensive detachment. 'And what is that?'

Ashley fixed huge emerald-green eyes accusingly on him. 'Each and every one of us has the capacity to go off the rails if the provocation is great enough. You once did so yourself, but I gather that I'm not supposed to remember that occasion.'

His golden features shuttered, his jawline clenching hard. 'The reminder is both unnecessary and irrelevant. I don't suffer from blackouts.'

In that split-second she came dangerously close to losing control. It had cost her dear to remind him of that last meeting. Rape? No, not rape. In bitter anger it had begun, and in savage passion it had ended. Not an act of love or even of desire. A final, humiliating expression of all-male contempt which had destroyed her pride for many, many months afterwards. Mastering her fury now was the hardest thing she had ever done and she only managed the feat by concentrating on her brother.

'I'd plead with you if I thought it would make any difference,' she admitted starkly.

'It wouldn't abate my anger one jot.'

Ashley thrust up her chin. 'OK. What about financial restitution?'

Vito dealt her a cold smile. 'Your family do not have the means. That "stupid fountain" you referred to was a sculpture, a quite irreplacable work of art. The car? A Ferrari F40 with one or two little extras custom-built to my requirements. I paid four hundred thousand pounds for it four years ago and it's already a collector's item.'

'Four h-hundred th-thousand pounds for a car?' Ashley stammered in disbelief.

'It was a limited edition put out to celebrate Ferrari's fortieth anniversary.'

'It's obscene...all that money for a car!' Ashley gasped helplessly. 'And the money means nothing to you!'

Vito shifted a lithely expressive hand. 'And everything to you.'

'Once we loved each other...' Every charged syllable hurt her throat, decimated her pride.

'Really?' Vito prompted. 'How strange that you should talk of love now when you made no reference to the emotion while we were together.'

Golden eyes dwelt unreadably on her hot cheeks and she evaded that appraisal. 'Can we stick to Tim?'

'You were the one who chose to stray into the past,' he reminded her.

'Only because I was stupid enough to try and appeal——'

'To some vein of sentimentality I might possess?' he guessed with derision. 'I'm not sentimental about sex.'

The assurance roared like a shockwave through her. She felt not only humiliated, she felt cheated. 'But you——'

'You destroyed what I felt for you.' It was an icy growl.

'You had a pretty similar effect on me!' she traded.

A dark, forbidding anger glimmered in his gaze. 'I actually believed that you would grow out of your ridiculous ideas. I actually honoured you with a proposal of marriage——'

'Oh, let's not make the mistake of referring to that offer in terms of honour!' Ashley flung back at him furiously. 'You made it painfully apparent that you thought you were doing me one very big favour. And you wanted a good excuse to avoid the gold-plated Plain Jane your parents kept on throwing at your head! That is, until you came to your senses and got your calculator out and snatched at her with both greedy hands!'

Without warning, Vito sprang up and strode forward to face her. His dark features were set like granite. 'If you ever refer to my late wife like that again, I may well choose to forget that you are a woman and give you the response that you truly deserve!'

'L-late? As in g-gone?' As he towered over her, six feet three inches of ferocious threat, she bowed her head, shattered by the news and cursing her impulsive tongue and the venom that could trip off it so easily in his radius. 'I'm sorry.'

'No, you're not,' Vito grated.

'All right. I can't really be sorry because I didn't know her!' Ashley slammed back at him with more truth than tact. 'But I'm sure she was a saint and a wonderful person, quite unlike me...'

'Most unlike you,' he breathed tautly in agreement. 'You have the face of a Botticelli angel, the temperament of a virago and the amorality of a natural whore. On no count do you have the smallest resemblance to Carina.'

Ashley had turned very pale, beads of perspiration dampening her brow. She was devastated by the vicious response she had invited. 'Dear God,' she muttered shakily. 'I must have been out of my mind when I got mixed up with you!'

A tiny pulse was beating in the hollow below one aristocratic cheekbone. 'We were both temporarily insane.'

Ashley slowly shook her head. Carina was dead. Carina was just a name and a face in a glossy magazine spread to her. It had been the wedding of the year in Italy, the amalgamation of two great fortunes. Vito hadn't wasted any time. One month after he had walked out on her, he had become engaged, and one month after that he had married. Carina had floated down the aisle, radiant in blinding white. And she had been radiant, ecstatically happy to have won Vito even by default. The bride had very obviously been in love.

However, Vito had married without love, without even the spur of sexual attraction. On their wedding night, Ashley had felt suicidal... the pain had been that bad, that unendurable. Until that day, she had been unable to bring herself to believe that he could actually go through with it.

But Vito had gone through with it. He had cut Ashley out of his life with terrifying immediacy and precision. And no regrets. Remembering still had the power to chill her to the marrow. She, who had once been so strong, had been broken like a toy and cast aside. She had learnt the hard way that she was no cleverer and no less vulnerable than any other woman in love. In the long, anguished months that had followed, she had lived in a kind of twilight world where she had co-existed with a ghost. In the end, she had been forced to confront and accept the most painful truth of all. Vito had never loved her. If he had, he couldn't have married another woman.

Stilling a reflexive shiver, she stared at his hand-stitched Italian leather shoes. He hates me, she thought weakly, he hates me because once he was foolish enough to ask me to marry him and I had the audacity to say no. Dear lord, how had this appalling confrontation developed? She was supposed to be here for Tim's benefit, wasn't she? And so far, she was guiltily aware that she had made a very poor showing.

'I'm sorry.' It stuck in her throat but she persisted for her brother's sake. 'I shouldn't have lost my temper.'

'Nobody ever taught you how to curb it,' Vito murmured harshly. 'But I could have.'

You and who else, mister? But the aggressive question remained sensibly unspoken. She felt like a volcano about to erupt. And she knew she couldn't. Only two people in the world had this effect on her. One was her father, the other was Vito. Rage took her over. Rage and fear. Instinctively she stifled her acknowledgement of that secondary emotion. Survival, to Ashley, meant never ever admitting that anything or anybody frightened her.

She cast him a glance in which desperate defiance and loathing mingled as blatantly as a blow. 'I'm not into crawling...'

A winged dark brow elevated. 'I wouldn't know. I've never seen you attempt such a feat.'

'But you'd like a ringside seat, wouldn't you?' She leapt upright, too restive to remain still, too threatened by his proximity to stay so close. The sudden movement dislodged the loose topknot which confined her hair and a curling tangle of Titian red rippled down far below her shoulders in shining disarray. Irritably she thrust the fiery strands back from her slanted cheekbones, accidentally intercepting a lingering stare from Vito as she lifted her head high. 'I know what you want to hear,' she said. 'I know what you're thinking right now. In fact, I'm pretty sure I know exactly what you've been thinking from the moment I walked into this room!'

'For the sake of peace, I hope not.' It was a low-pitched growl which made the sensitive skin at the nape of her neck prickle.

His intonation threw her off balance for a second. Intent golden eyes watched her still with the grace of a gazelle in flight, sunlight glittering fire in that amazing curtain of vibrant hair. Her return look was blank.

'You want to hear that I deeply regret not marrying you,' she stated with characteristic bluntness.

'Do I?' Vito didn't move a muscle.

She squared her shoulders, hoping that he was bigger than his fragile male ego when the cards were down. 'I have to be honest so that we can get this hangover from four years ago out of the way.'

'Oh, please be honest, *cara*,' he encouraged lazily.

She swallowed hard. 'If you must know, I'm still proud of the fact that I refused to become your possession. A life of round-the-clock surveillance and subjugation at your hands would have stifled me. It would never have worked.'

'It worked in bed. *Dio*,' Vito interposed in a sizzling undertone, 'how it worked...'

Fierce heat pooled in the pit of her stomach. Flustered and embarrassed out of all proportion to the remark, she said nothing.

Vito surveyed her with formidable cool. The chill factor in the air was powerful. 'It would have been such a sacrifice? To be my wife? To wear silk next to your skin, diamonds at your throat? I valued you far beyond your true worth.'

'Well, if you have to think like a tradesman in enumerating the material advantages I missed out on, I expect you did,' Ashley parried between clenched teeth. 'But you knew from the start how I felt about marriage. You can't say you weren't warned. Marriage is a patriarchal institution which benefits men and oppresses women. It conditions my sex into dependence and passivity, lowers their status and deprives them of individuality.'

'Feminist claptrap. *Dio*. I've never heard so much rubbish!' Vito raked back at her in a lion's roar of intimidation.

Her breasts swelled with anger. Jerkily she shrugged. 'You are, naturally, entitled to your own opinion—as I am entitled to mine. In any case, I'm not here to resurrect a past that we'd both prefer to forget. Why can't we leave personalities out of this? I didn't come here to antagonise you. You make me say things I don't mean to say. You always did,' she completed accusingly.

'You apologise with such finesse.'

In a passion of frustrated emotion, she whirled away. It had been a long time since she had voiced the beliefs she had first formed in her early teens. For some inexplicable reason, she didn't feel the same religious fervour of conviction that she had once had. But that scarcely mattered now. Why should she apologise for saving them both from the long-drawn-out agonies of a disastrous marriage?

After five months, they had been at each other's throats at least twice a day. Near the end, it had been like living on the edge of a precipice when you had a pronounced fear of heights. Tears stung her eyes. She was the one person who could reason with Vito on Tim's behalf and yet she was the very worst messenger he could have had.

Time had not lessened Vito's antipathy. She stole a covert glance at his rock-hard profile, absorbing the innate ruthlessness stamped into every slashing line of his stark bone-structure. No, they could never have parted friends. Vito came from a long line of blue-blooded, immensely wealthy and arrogant people. Negative responses had figured rarely in his experiences. Everything he wanted, he got. Everything he wished, happened. When your name was Cavalieri, the world was your oyster and the pearl at the centre was always yours. That Vito had been prepared to marry her in the very teeth of his family's opposition had made her flat refusal all the more heinous a crime in his eyes.

'If you could just bring yourself to withdraw the complaint against Tim,' she pleaded tightly.

'Why would I do that?' Vito fielded drily. 'If I think like a tradesman, I would obviously be striking a most unequal bargain. Freeing your brother from the punishment he most assuredly deserves would not fill me with any warm feeling of benevolence. His freedom is worth nothing to me. What is it worth to you?'

The casual enquiry struck her as savagely cruel. She trembled. 'Anything...everything,' she whispered, thinking of Tim's smashed future and her mother's fragile mental stability and the unending guilt which would be hers alone if she could not persuade Vito to change his mind.

'Is it worth your own freedom?'

Her delicately pointed profile turned to him. 'I don't understand.'

Black-lashed golden eyes flamed over her tense figure, skimming across the feminine curves that even the unflattering clothing could not disguise and finally fanning at an outrageously leisurely pace back up to her burning cheeks. Only a hot-blooded Italian could have projected that much sexual menace into a single look. 'Anything…everything? Intriguing,' he murmured softly. 'If you returned to my bed, it is possible that I might be persuaded to withdraw the complaint.'

Her slim hands closed convulsively together, the heated colour draining from her complexion. 'That's not funny, Vito.'

'It wasn't intended to be.' He sank down with inherent grace on the edge of his immaculately tidy desk. 'You come to me on my terms—entirely on my terms,' he stressed, 'and your brother goes free.'

'That's obscene!' Ashley gasped.

'You shared my bed once without love. You could surely share it just as happily with hatred,' he drawled.

Her hands parted and knotted into balled fists.

'Your body language is so uniquely expressive,' Vito remarked. 'Bring some of that fire into the bedroom and I might even be persuaded to buy your delinquent brother a Ferrari of his own.'

She shuddered with rage, fought the emotion and won only by dint of trapping her tongue painfully between her teeth. How dared he? How dared he send her up like this? For, of course, that was what he was doing. He was settling old scores. He wanted to humiliate her. In the situation she was in, it was inhumanly cruel. But that was Vito. The dark side of Vito. The ruthless, unrelentingly vengeful side of Vito which she had clashed with unforgettably on the day he'd married another woman.

He flung his dark head back and laughed soft and deep in his throat. He was utterly pagan in his unashamed enjoyment of her mortification. '*Allora, cara.* Once you said to me, "If you feel like it, go for it". I am, as you so succinctly advised, going for it.'

'But you can't be serious...you can't be,' she stammered.

Glittering dark eyes rested on her with a fierce, wholly physical intensity. 'It would have to be marriage...'

'Why the hell would you want to marry me now?' she blistered back at him, abruptly relocating the power of proper speech.

A satiric smile slanted his expressive mouth. 'But you know the answer to that question, *cara*,' he said smoothly. 'You told me why four years ago. I want a servant to pick up after me, a devoted slave to massage my ego and a bimbo to show off in designer clothes. And, last but not least, sex...unlimited sex, whenever I want it. Only marriage could supply me with all these essentials.'

Involuntarily her jaw dropped, oxygen escaping her lungs in a shattered sound of disbelief. She had long since forgotten those bitter words. Vito, she registered with a sinking sensation in the pit of her stomach, had not.

'In addition,' he continued, luxuriant lashes dropping reflectively low as he looked her over again with incredibly offensive thoroughness, 'beneath that ridiculous miniature terrorist outfit you sport lurks a perfect body and a very beautiful woman. I still want to possess that woman. And why should I not when the means are within my grasp?'

'You're crazy!' she cried. 'Absolutely stark, staring mad!'

'Am I?' Vito surveyed her with a brand of cold, grim satisfaction that made her skin crawl. 'Are you telling me that I could get you any other way? I want you, Ashley. That is the only card you have to play. Whether or not you choose to play it is entirely up to you.'

'I'd sooner be dead than married to you!' Stinging conviction lanced from every biting syllable.

'Is that your final answer?'

In three enraged steps, Ashley reached the door and swung helplessly round to vent yet another last word.

'You vengeful bastard!' she hissed in disgust. 'I hope you burn in hell for what you've said to me today!'

'And I would warn you that "where two raging fires meet together, they do consume the thing that feeds their fury".' Contemptuous amusement glittered in his unyielding gaze as he absorbed her bewilderment. 'Haven't you ever read *The Taming of the Shrew*, Ashley?'

In her desperate haste to depart, she cannoned into the stalwart solidarity of his secretary, who was hovering anxiously outside. 'How can you work for a chauvinistic, woman-hating swine like that?' she demanded shrilly on her way past.

CHAPTER THREE

'UNLIMITED sex, whenever I want it...' Ashley's teeth ground audibly together as she elbowed her passage out of the lift. Seething over the treatment she had received, she stalked from the building. How dared he speak to her like that? How *dared* he?

Well, you did what you could and you failed, she told herself bracingly. Tim's stricken face lurched into her conscience. Missing her step, she stumbled and nearly fell, horror darkening her eyes. And it was there, right there in the middle of the crowded pavement with people pushing past her on either side, that the harsh reality of Tim's predicament finally struck home hard. Her self-righteous fury evaporated, leaving her limp and shaken.

Dear heaven, was she actually planning to stand back and watch her kid brother go to prison? Guilt swallowed her alive. Vito had at least agreed to see her. And what had she done with that opportunity? Instead of pursuing Tim's cause with suitable tact and humility, she had gone off on an emotional tangent, dredging up personal issues which had had no place in the dialogue. She had blown Tim's one hope of freedom, wilfully, recklessly blown it for the selfish satisfaction of provoking Vito.

Her stomach gave a nauseous lurch. With so much at stake, only a lunatic would have behaved as she had. It was useless to plead that she could never have foreseen this sequence of events... it did not make her any less responsible for the results.

Tim had defended her. And in her name he had been baited, beaten up and humiliated. Tormented by his inability to silence Pietro, Tim's rage and resentment had inevitably centred on Vito, the male he viewed as the author of all his sister's misfortunes. He had probably intended to drive Vito's Ferrari away and leave it somewhere, giving Vito a scare. Ashley was absolutely certain that Tim had not meant to damage it. Like most teenage boys, Tim was car-crazy. The wanton destruction of such an exclusive car would have been beyond him.

Ashley was convinced that, filled with Dutch courage and fired by an adolescent desire for the only revenge within his reach, Tim had embarked on a stupid, boyish prank that had concluded in the kind of disaster he could not have dreamt up in his worst nightmares. But no court would view his outrageous conduct in such a mellow light. The court would not hear about the provocation Tim had endured for so many weeks beforehand either. Hadn't Tim already suffered enough? 'Aren't you responsible for everything that drags our family down?' Susan had condemned bitterly. All of a sudden the stark truth of that accusation seemed cruelly apt.

You break the rules, you pay the price. Four years ago, she had moved into Vito's apartment, well aware that she was contravening her father's staunchly moral principles. Faced with his fury, she had refused to hang her head in shame. She had been defiant to the last and in the end she had paid a high price for that defiance, but it had occurred to her recently that she had not been the only one to pay that price.

The scant references Tim had made to that period of their lives had made it painfully obvious that her behaviour had caused her mother tremendous distress. And what her mother had endured then would be as nothing to what she would endure at the mere thought of the son she idolised going to prison. Emotionally fragile as she was at the best of times, it was very possible that the crisis would push Sylvia Forrester into another breakdown. That danger was as unthinkable to Ashley as the risk of her little brother ending up in a cell, and the means to defeat both threats were, she registered dully, within her own hands.

Was it too late? Ashley straightened her shoulders and breathed in as she turned in her tracks. She had to dig very deep for the courage to walk back into the Cavalieri Bank. Hot-cheeked, she approached the reception desk, inwardly cringing at the necessity. One of the receptionists approached her. 'Mr di Cavalieri phoned down to say that you could go straight up, Miss Forrester.'

In bewilderment, Ashley blinked. How could Vito possibly be expecting her? How could he have known that she would return before she knew it herself?

In the lift she fancied that she felt the weight of a ball and chain on her ankle. Pacing down that wide corridor again, she imagined she could hear the clank of the heavy links as Vito rattled her chain. But already her agile brain was working back over their previous dialogue with greater cool.

It didn't make sense. It didn't make sense that Vito should demand that she marry him. Vito was highly sexed but he was no slave to that sex-drive. He had proved that fact when he walked away to marry another woman, disdaining any attempt to continue a relationship in which marriage would not be the end result. Furthermore, so much bitterness lay between them now—how could he possibly still find her desirable? Was it true after all, that old cliché which said that men were different, more easily able to separate all emotion from the physical? Was Vito playing some sort of crazy power game with her?

He was a tall, lithe silhouette by the tinted wall of glass that filtered light into the ultra-modern room. He contemplated her in silence. What lay behind those impassive dark eyes was anybody's guess. But suddenly she was aware as she had not allowed herself to be aware earlier that she was facing a brilliant adversary, infinitely more experienced in tactical warfare than she was.

'How did you know that I'd come back?' she prompted when it seemed to her that the nailbiting silence might soon contrive to suffocate her if she didn't break it.

An eloquent dark brow lifted. 'The fury, the walkout, the truculent reappearance? The pattern is not unfamiliar to me.'

Burning colour drenched her pallor. 'You've got me over a barrel.'

'Crude,' he acknowledged. 'But apparently true. I never credited you with so much family feeling.'

She evaded his scrutiny, conscious that he might believe he had some grounds to betray surprise on that point. In the past, she had strenuously resisted his desire to meet her family and had inevitably been forced to behave as though family ties were unimportant to her. But how could she have taken him home to witness at first hand the atmosphere in her own home? How would he have reacted to the discovery that her father loathed all foreigners? Her father had more prejudices than a roomful of people could acquire between them in a lifetime. Vito would have been politely appalled and she would have cringed with embarrassment. The difference in their backgrounds would have been even more mortifyingly apparent.

'What possible pleasure could you receive from forcing me into marriage?' she demanded in helpless frustration.

'What force do I employ? You have the gift of free choice.'

'That's not fair!' she argued in growing desperation.

'Life isn't always fair.'

'You're demanding the impossible!'

'Then we have nothing further to discuss.' It was said with cool finality.

'We could talk about this,' she proffered curtly, playing for time.

'We have a great deal to talk about. We'll lunch at my apartment.'

Thrown by the suggestion, she stared up at him. 'Lunch?'

'I'm hungry.' Vito was already shrugging his magnificent physique into a superb cashmere coat. Perfect calm and sublime insouciance blended in the graceful lift of one ebony brow.

'I thought you had a house here now.'

'The apartment is more convenient during working hours.'

A private lift ran from his office suite down to an underground car park where a car awaited them. 'So... what are you in?' Vito enquired as the limousine nosed a forceful passage out into the slow moving traffic. 'Your brother was not disposed to satisfy my curiosity on the evening that we met.'

'In?' she repeated uncertainly.

'Your career,' he clarified with impatience. 'The career that you chose in place of me.'

'Oh.' Studying her tightly linked hands, she paled and decided to lie. 'The retail trade.' It wasn't entirely a lie, she reasoned. Until she had obtained some qualifications in child-care at evening classes, she had been employed at a large department store.

'You surprise me. It was not the field I believed you would choose. I assumed you would choose something more high-profile.'

She shrugged, evading his sardonic scrutiny. No, she couldn't tell him. It would be the ultimate humiliation. How could he guess? she reasoned frantically. Had she completed her course in accountancy, this would only have been her first year in paid employment. Vito would scarcely be looking for the trappings of success. Why should she tell him that he had been right all along? Right to say that she was on the wrong course? Right to suspect that at heart she had neither the interest in the subject nor the natural affinity with figures to shine in that field?

She had gone against everybody's advice when she'd chosen accountancy. But she had been determined to go into business and childishly, hopelessly set on proving to her father that she could succeed in a discipline dominated by the male sex. Stubborn as she was, she had had to fail before she could face the truth, although she still believed that if it hadn't been for Vito deserting her the month before her exams started and the subsequent trauma of her pregnancy, she would at least have passed those exams.

She loved working with young children. That was a natural inclination which she had rigorously suppressed throughout her teens, deeming such employment as one more little womanly pursuit which she was too clever to fall into. Now the world had turned full circle for her. She was studying part-time for a degree with the hope that eventually she would be able to train as a teacher. And all that, she realised abruptly, was about to end. The life which she had painstakingly put together again for herself would be destroyed a second time, for no greater reason than a barbarously male need for revenge.

'Are there likely to be any contractual problems concerning your release from employment?'

'None.' She was briefly amused by the idea of the day nursery where she worked pulling out all the plugs to retain one humble employee. 'But I still don't see why you should want to marry me.'

'I have a strong motivation which I haven't shared with you yet,' Vito conceded, shooting her a veiled glance. 'I believe you may be relieved when you hear it.'

Curiosity flickered. 'Tell me now.'

'I prefer the greater privacy of the apartment.'

The apartment was mercifully not the one which they had once shared. It was smaller, more formally furnished and clearly designed only for occasional occupation, but a trio of Toulouse Lautrec pencil drawings still hung in the elegant dining-room for equally occasional appreciation. Ashley was quite certain they were originals. A Cavalieri with a world-renowned private art collection would not be satisfied with anything less. At a rough estimate those drawings had to be worth well over a million pounds.

The fish-out-of-water sensation she had often experienced in Vito's radius four years previously returned to haunt her. This was not her world. The daughter of a

man who ran a car dealership did not belong in such a
rarified milieu, and if she had ever thought otherwise
she had once received firm confirmation of her unsuit-
ability from another Cavalieri. Not Vito... his mother.
With the discipline of long practice she suppressed that
most degrading memory. Somewhere she still had the
cheque Elena di Cavalieri had left behind.

A manservant served the meal. Although Ashley had
scarcely eaten from the hour of Tim's arrest, she could
only manage to push the food round her plate and sip
at the wine. Vito, on the other hand, worked with well-
bred restraint and no lack of appetite through each light
course, unperturbed by her stony response to his con-
versational sallies.

Coffee was served in the spacious lounge. Ashley flung
herself down on a feather-stuffed sofa. 'Well, let's hear
it, then,' she invited, tilting her chin in an upward thrust,
'this strong motivation for wanting to marry me that
required greater privacy.'

'Naturally I'm not considering a lifetime commitment,' Vito asserted from his stance by the fireplace.
'But it has occurred to me that you could well be worth
every pound your brother has cost me and more.'

'How?' she demanded baldly, tension tightening her
muscles; she hadn't a clue what he could be driving at
and she hated the sensation of being in the dark. It
seemed that she had been right. Clearly Vito did have a
more devious reason than rampant desire for the outrageous demand that they unite in holy wedlock—unholy
wedlock, she adjusted inwardly, reflecting on the sheer
frequency and violence with which they had fought in
the past.

Vito continued to study her with curiously intent
golden eyes. 'There is only one thing in life I really want
which fate has so far denied me.'

'The British Crown Jewels?' Ashley gibed. 'I can't
think of much else that you couldn't contrive to buy.'

'I want a child,' Vito imparted, as if she hadn't made
that facetious remark.

The announcement hit her like a punch in the gut. It turned her to stone, freezing her usually expressive face, but she could feel the blood slowly draining away from below her skin, the sudden mad thump of an accelerated heartbeat and a twisting pulling of pain deep down in her stomach.

Could he know...could he possibly know about the child she had miscarried? A shred of sanity returned to soothe her. There was absolutely no way that Vito could know about her pregnancy back then.

'You don't have any children?' She had to force the question from between dry, strained lips. For the past four years she had rigidly refused to think about the fact that Vito would most assuredly be fathering the children he had always admitted he wanted with another woman, the children she had flatly refused even to consider having with him.

'Six months after our marriage, Carina became ill,' Vito volunteered with visible reluctance. 'She had leukaemia. With the treatment involved there was naturally no question of even attempting to conceive a child.'

Ashley was shattered. In the midst of her current plight, it had not even occurred to her to wonder how so young a woman had died, but she had dimly assumed it might have been a car accident, something like that. This was entirely different. 'I'm sorry,' she whispered dazedly, still too confused to put together what he was telling her.

'Why should you be?'

'Because I'm not a totally unfeeling bitch!' Ashley lanced back at him furiously. 'Is my sympathy less acceptable than other people's?'

Pale beneath his dark skin, Vito released his breath in a hiss. 'Yes,' he admitted. 'Somehow it is.'

She was trying to put together what he had so far said. A glimmer of the truth threatened and she thrust it away, unable to believe that her own reasoning was leading her in the right direction. 'What,' she began a little unsteadily, 'has the fact that you want a child got to do with me?'

'I'm prepared to marry you so that you can give me that child.'

Ashley slid slowly upright in a movement lacking her usual supple grace. A dark, deep flush had overlaid her translucent skin. 'You're insane!' she gasped.

'I don't see why it should be so impossible a request. It's certainly not insane,' Vito countered. 'You're absolutely perfect for the role of surrogate mother. You don't want children of your own. After the child was born we would divorce and you would be free to continue your life as you wish without any interference from me.'

Ashley raked a shaking hand through her tousled hair and stared at him, wild-eyed with disbelief. 'I don't believe I'm hearing this. It's the most obscene suggestion I've ever heard! You could go out there and marry any one of a dozen women, I'm quite sure, and have a family the same way anyone else does!'

'But I don't want another wife.' Vito cast her a grim smile. 'Not a "forever and ever" wife. It would be wickedly unfair of me to marry another woman purely and simply to have a child. I could not sustain such an empty pretence of a relationship——'

'But you evidently don't consider it wickedly unfair to do that to me!' Ashley interrupted tempestuously.

'There would be no pretences in our relationship and, in any case, you are scarcely in the normal run of your sex. You don't even like children. You have never had any intention of tying yourself down to such a responsibility or of risking your career by taking time out to have a family. You told me all that quite unforgettably four years ago.'

She wanted to scream at him that she had been nineteen years old and as opinionated and untried in her convictions as most teenagers were. Her shrinking distaste from the very idea of pregnancy had been formed while she watched her mother's health dragged down by a countless succession of miscarriages in pursuit of the son her father had been so selfishly determined to have.

'You have years ahead of you in which you could marry again,' she flung at him tautly.

'But I may never meet someone I wish to marry. Apart from that possibility,' Vito rejoined, 'I have no desire to be an elderly father. My father was nearly fifty when I was born, and now he's dead. We were never close. There was too big an age-gap.'

He had never told her that his father had been so much older. Elena di Cavalieri must have been at least thirty years her husband's junior. Ashley's mind shifted away from the side-issue, which was so much more easy to consider than the absolutely impossible proposition Vito was putting before her. A hysterical laugh fluttered in her throat. Dear God, if only he knew that he had so nearly become... but then, it hadn't been so nearly, she reminded herself, thinking of how tragically short-lived her pregnancy had been and then reflecting in the same almost hysterical vein that, if Vito knew the female gynaecological history of her family, she would be the very last woman he would have approached with such a demand!

'I never dreamt you would even consider me worthy of such an honour as providing you with an heir,' Ashley delivered, terrified that her perilously thin control would splinter into shards in front of him. 'Not with the opinion you have of me.'

Vito's hard mouth tightened. 'You are physically very attractive, mentally very bright, and morally very courageous.'

Ashley was beginning to shake. 'You mean I score straight As as a potential cuckoo-type mother but fail all along the line as a woman!'

'I don't believe I said that.' Vito watched her with veiled eyes.

'But that's what you meant!' Ashley lashed back at him painfully. 'You think a real woman puts a man before everything else in her life, including herself!'

'All I do know is that in your case,' Vito breathed harshly, 'I was not the man capable of persuading you to make the smallest compromise or sacrifice on my behalf.'

Ashley loosed a high-pitched laugh. 'A small compromise? A small sacrifice?' she echoed. 'Move to Italy, give up my studies and all hope of ever having an independent career, marry you against my most basic instincts and then proceed to produce progeny with rabbit-like efficiency! All those months you pretended that you understood how I felt——'

'I was being remarkably patient and tactful,' Vito incised.

'You were being bloody devious and dishonest!' Ashley countered.

'I was compromising my own convictions in an attempt to save our relationship,' Vito bit out between clenched teeth. 'There were times I wanted to shake you until your teeth rattled! There were times I wanted to use physical force to make you listen to me! Times I wanted to get inside your head and rearrange the circuitry into some form of normality——'

'I always said the only sort of real woman you could cope with would be a housekeeping robot!' Ashley spat, grabbing up her bag. 'I've had enough of this, and I wouldn't like to tell you exactly what I think of your baby-boom proposition, although I would dearly like to tell you what to do with it!'

'You walk out of that door and your brother goes to prison!'

Ashley froze with her hand reaching out towards the door and slowly swung back. 'You bastard!' she gasped strickenly, recalled to reality again with a nasty jerk when for a few minutes there it had almost been like old times, when they had fought hammer and tongs, no insult too low to be utilised, no theme too sensitive to employ.

'I am what you made me,' Vito responded very softly, a dark brilliance simmering like the start of a summer storm in the back of his fierce gaze. 'The guy who gave you fabulous sex but no deeply unsatisfied longing for a permanent commitment.'

Ashley snatched up her abandoned coffee-cup and threw it at him with an unrepeatable word. 'How dare you talk to me like that?' she seethed.

The cup smashed harmlessly against the edge of the fireplace but the contents spattered Vito's jacket. It served him right, Ashley thought furiously. Vito had always seemed to have the opinion that it was somehow beneath him to duck when she threw things.

'You know, my father once assured me that a gentleman never hits a lady,' Vito murmured half under his breath. 'Therefore I should feel quite free to retaliate. After all, there is no individual worthy of the title of a lady currently in this room.'

'You lay a finger on——' Ashley broke off as a quiet knock on the door prefaced the entry of the manservant with the offer of a second cup of coffee.

'Thank you,' Vito stated straight-faced. 'But I've had all the coffee I can handle.'

As the door shut, a powerful hand closed round one of Ashley's wrists and yanked her bodily forward, her slender five-foot-two-inch figure suddenly twisting away from his proximity in dismay.

'Let go of me!' she seethed, and when her demand was ignored something snapped inside her. Determined to break that controlling hold, she went wild, arms flailing, legs kicking. Vito lifted her off her feet with frightening strength, shook her once in mid-air, making her feel maddeningly like a rag doll, and brought her down again in a similarly controlled landing.

'If you want to behave like a wild animal,' Vito intoned in even addition, 'I will be more than happy to supply you with a cage.'

Shocked and winded by the merciless speed of his response, she clashed with glittering golden eyes. The collision left her breathless. The final token struggle, she conceded dully, was over. Not surprisingly, she had lost. She had never won many points with Vito. If she was

strong-willed and stubborn, Vito was doubly so. With a
knife at his throat, Vito would disdain retreat. His temperament was as fiery as her own but his was controlled
by the cool of intellect, not by passion. And in any confrontation he would always triumph on the ruthless edge
of that streak of cruelty that was uniquely his. And now
it seemed that he had her precisely where he had always
wanted her...absolutely and irrevocably within his power.

Abruptly her thought-train was broken by the
awareness that Vito had not yet freed her from his hold.
Forced into rawly intimate acquaintance with every sleek,
hard angle of his lean, muscular length, she attempted
to edge out of reach. An imprisoning hand splayed across
her hipbone, reinforcing the physical contact she was
suddenly desperate to avoid.

'Leave me alone!' she demanded wildly.

Ruthless fingers knotted and twisted into the tangled
fall of her hair, tipping her head back.

'You're behaving like an——'

'An aroused male?' Vito vented a low-pitched laugh
that did something inexcusable to the level of support
offered by her knees. 'But I am. Very aroused.'

'V-Vito...no!' But he had already pressed his mouth
hotly to the tiny pulse flickering wildly in the hollow of
her throat and she moaned, beginning to tremble like
someone caught unexpectedly in a violent storm. Somewhere in the bemused reaches of her brain she was recalling that she had this one weak spot where Vito was
concerned. When he touched her...oh, God, when he
touched her! The tip of his tongue delved provocatively
between her mutinously closed lips and withdrew again.

A choked whimper broke low in her throat, sudden
raw and delicious tension of a different kind jerking her
every muscle tight, driving every single rational thought
from her swimming head.

Involuntarily her whole body was reaching up and out,
reacting to the lure of an anticipation that dug painful
claws of need into her flesh. Slowly, unbearably slowly,
so that her hands clutched pleadingly at his broad

shoulders, he brought his mouth down to the now opened invitation of hers.

He kissed the same way he made love: with fire and passion and unholy sexual intensity. Her every skin cell came alive in one gigantic whoosh of feeling. Her skin was clammy, her breasts were swelling and her nipples were pinching into aching tightness. Liquidity ran in a river of drowning weakness through her limbs and she would have sagged if he hadn't been holding her upright. For long timeless moments, she was in a hot, swirling darkness where only the primitive demands of her own body held sway. He moved against her, lithely erotic as a jungle cat, letting her feel the thrusting evidence of his masculinity. She gave up on the unequal fight and folded into the heat and hardness of him, abandoning herself to the savage potency of his hunger as he swept her off her feet and carried her out of the room.

'Take the rest of the day off.'

She heard that. She heard him speaking to someone. That penetrated the haze of passion even as she registered that Vito sounded most unlike his usual cool, controlled self. Some physical sense of where she was penetrated as he brought her down on some unyielding horizontal surface, and her eyes flew wide open, trained to his darkly handsome face above hers, taut and flushed and determined with the force of a hunger she too well understood.

'It's like the first time all over again,' Vito swore huskily. 'Except this time you still have too many clothes on.'

After an arrested pause, Ashley stared up at him in horror, delivered from the voracious grip of passion by a deluge of powerful emotions. Caressing fingertips were exploring beneath her T-shirt, and, before she could quench it, her body betrayed her all over again. A long sobbing sigh escaped her as he shaped her breasts, an expert thumb teasing at the sensitive peak of her engorged flesh.

Attacked simultaneously by the extremities of shock,
disbelief and a cringing sense of shame, Ashley froze.
She was too devastated to cope with anything beyond
her own reactions to what had just happened between
them. The impossible...the unmentionable...the unforgivable. She wasn't a teenager with overactive hormones any more. How could she let him do this to her?
In unwitting anguish, she looked up at him, seeking an
answer to the inexplicable.

Vito's hands slowly stilled, virtually unnoticed by her.
'It hasn't changed, has it, *cara*? We have an insatiable
hunger for each other. Something so powerful I didn't
even believe it existed until I met you. That wasn't
enough for me the last time,' he breathed in an unsteady
undertone. 'But this time, it's going to be the icing on
the cake.'

'Don't be disgusting!' Ashley made another feeble attempt to dislodge herself from his hold so that she could
rearrange her disordered clothing. Little tremors of
physical after-shock were still quaking through her, nor
was she yet in any fit state to deal with the ramifications
of her own failure to maintain control of the situation.

'And what a relief it is to be with a woman who believes she can treat sex as casually as a man, who expects
none of the traditional touches of courtship and romance and who would certainly never dream of demanding that I do something as boringly conventional
as wait until *after* the wedding,' Vito continued smoothly.

Something perilously close to naked panic assailed her
in the wake of that most enlightening speech.

'Something wrong?' Lustrous dark eyes were tracking
her every change of expression with the efficiency of a
scanner tuning in to easily read airwaves.

An awful lot of somethings. So many that she couldn't
put them all together at once. Without the smallest
preparation she was being confronted with all the false
images she had put up for Vito's benefit four years ago,
when it had seemed so desperately important that he did
not wring an admission of undying love from her. Being

loved gave immense power to the loved one. Her father had wielded that power over her mother throughout their marriage. Ashley had been determined that Vito would never receive that weapon from her.

It's chemistry, it's my age, it's infatuation, she had told herself then. I do not love him, I do not need him, I will not look for him when he is not there. That had been her mantra of self-defence. And she had behaved accordingly, refusing verbally to grant him the exclusive commitment he demanded and loudly disclaiming the double standards which made sexual experimentation acceptable for a man but not for a woman.

Certainly she had not behaved that way without some justification. And from the outset Vito had had that exclusive commitment whether he had chosen to believe it or not. But Vito had acted as though he owned her. She had played her role with the nervous defiance of someone being beaten back into an increasingly tight corner by an overpoweringly masculine male, who thought liberation was something to do with occupied territories and absolutely nothing to do with the female sex. Looking at Vito now, so cool and so calm, it was hard to recall the furious violence of their arguments and the ferocious jealousy and possessiveness he had demonstrated when she dared to show him that he did not have the right to dictate her every move.

'Vito...I...' It occurred to her that all those proud pretences of hers had truly come home to roost with her now. Vito had an utterly mistaken impression of her true character. Vito had always had a most unendearing habit of misinterpreting what she said, especially when she flung things she didn't mean in a temper. And now, not unnaturally, Vito expected her to practise what she had once so loudly preached.

'"If you feel like it, go for it,"' Vito challenged in an accented drawl as smooth as black velvet. 'And you can't say that you don't feel like making love because I already know that you do.'

'I wish you'd stop throwing every s-stupid thing I ever said back at me!' she launched and subsided again as a blunt forefinger skimmed across her midriff and lingered just above her waistband.

'So you admit that some of it was stupid,' Vito probed mercilessly. 'Or is it just that you would admit to anything sooner than share this bed with me right now?'

In despair she turned her head away, wondering dully if sharing his bed now was Vito's callous method of sealing the bargain she had yet to agree to or merely the first in a long line of heartless humiliations, designed to reduce her pride to rubble. Dear God, if her brother's freedom was to hinge on this, what was she to do? If Vito made that demand now, she felt that she would walk out of this apartment and under the nearest bus, because she would never be able to look either him or herself in the face again.

'I've never been promiscuous,' she mumbled.

Vito dealt her pinched profile a grimly amused smile. Had she seen it, rage would have revived her, but she did not see it. Nor did it occur to her that Vito was being astoundingly patient for a male bent on immediately slaking his lust.

And, without warning, what she was to do was taken care of in the most unwelcome fashion possible. Forty-eight hours of frantic worry, powered by insufficient sleep and food, abruptly took their toll. Ashley burst into floods of tears, shocking herself as much as she shocked him. Her most pressing need then was for privacy but Vito caught her back before she could reel off the bed.

'Let go!' she sobbed.

'How can I?' He tugged her into his arms.

'I can't take any more!' Blinded by the raining gush of tears, sobs wrenched at her throat. 'I'm . . . I'm not a c-call girl or something.'

'No, you have entirely the wrong attitude and far too much class,' Vito assured her instantly, encouraging her to weep all over his shirt-front while he smoothed her tousled hair back from her brow.

'I c-can't cope with you right now and you know it!' In a surge of mortified frustration, she struck weakly at his solidity with a loosely coiled fist. 'I n-never cry! I despise w-women who do this!'

He murmured incomprehensibly soothing things in Italian. She cried even harder because, God help her, she liked it. The scent of warm male flesh, so achingly familiar, enveloped her and was as strangely reassuring as the rock-steady beat of his heart. She couldn't remember when anyone had last put their arms round her... it had probably been him. Something akin to despair engulfed her, adding to her bitter burden of defeat.

A cruising forefinger drifted confidently down over one damp cheek. She didn't move. She was comfortable, comforted, and as he deftly eased her on to the sofa at the foot of the bed she burrowed unconsciously closer. Physically and mentally drained by complete exhaustion, she refused to question the incongruity of her behaviour.

'I should apologise.' Vito hesitated. 'Sometimes you bring out something in me that I don't like very much.'

'That makes two of us. You must see how utterly hopeless it is to expect me to——'

Long fingers tipped up her face. A faintly chilling smile slanted his mouth. 'Don't fight me.' Dark eyes held hers by sheer force of will. 'If you fight me, you'll get hurt.'

'Do you always kick people when they're down?'

'You're not down.' He stood up. 'You're just recharging your batteries. I suggest you move into this apartment while I'm away.'

'Away?'

'I'm leaving for Geneva in a couple of hours. I'll be back next week. Maybe I'll take you to the opera. You like the opera,' he reminded her with the attitude of someone presenting a sulky child with a consolation prize.

She gritted her teeth. 'Tim?'

'I will contact the police.'

'They mightn't listen.'

'The entire episode took place on private property. Whether I choose to prosecute or not is my business,' Vito pointed out with inborn arrogance.

A shuddering spasm of relief slivered through her. He had done this to her, she realised fearfully, encouraged her to dash herself to pieces against that absolute obduracy that was his greatest strength. Four years ago, he had ripped her to shreds by the simple act of walking out. A giant black chasm had opened below her feet and she had drowned. But while she had drowned in the emptiness, the loneliness and the savage agony of loss, Vito had been getting married and moving on coolly to put together the kind of brilliant deals which had made his name in the circles of international finance, his eventual reward that of becoming the youngest ever president of the Cavalieri Mercantile Bank. There was a lesson to be learned in that comparison and it terrified her.

Maybe she was paranoid, maybe it was her over-active imagination, but she had the horrible suspicion that each and every one of her experiences today had been exactly choreographed with the precise intention of reducing her to her current level of emotional devastation.

'I'll make you a lousy wife, Vito,' she whispered.

'"*Rien ne chatouille qui ne pince*".'

Her French wasn't up to the translation.

'Montaigne,' Vito supplied. '"Nothing gives pleasure but that which gives pain".'

'I'm not a masochist,' she said dully.

'Think of it as a business arrangement—an exchange of mutual benefit. If you endeavour not to be a lousy wife, I will endeavour not to be a lousy husband. What happens between us after the wedding will therefore be your responsibility.'

'Oh, neat cop-out, Vito!' Ashley flung him a glance of weary scorn. He was already pressing a button on the cordless phone, ordering the car to be brought round, impervious, it seemed, to her attitude.

'To all intents and purposes it will be a normal marriage.'

'If we lived in a lunatic asylum, I guess it would be.'

He cast her a genuinely amused smile. The immense charm he was capable of sprang out at her for the first time that day. Involuntarily her gaze clung to his, zapped by that almost forgotten power-surge. 'I knew it wouldn't take long for your batteries to pick up again. Oh, yes, before you go,' he drawled. 'One more little thing. Ground rules.'

'I beg your pardon?'

'I believe in highlighting the small print of any contract with an unwary partner,' Vito asserted. 'I expect you to be pleasant to my family. I will also expect you to dress in a manner appropriate to your status. We'll sort that out next week.'

Her teeth gritted, her lips firmly compressed.

Vito stilled. 'And, last but not least, no men,' he added very, very quietly. 'No flirtations, no male friends, platonic or otherwise. If you break that rule, life won't be worth living, I assure you, *cara*.'

Her sensitive stomach executed a nervous somersault.

CHAPTER FOUR

'YOU actually want me to believe that you're grateful I brought you two guys together again?' Tim uttered a rude word of disbelief but Ashley could see in his eyes that, yes, that was what her kid brother so desperately wanted to believe, because that way he could enjoy his continuing freedom with an almost clear conscience.

Ashley wished that his train would come. They had been over and over the same ground repeatedly in the past five days. Like her, Tim had a suspicious nature. Unlike Susan, he had not been content simply to accept her story at face value. It had also taken considerable persistence to dissuade Tim from his original intent of seeing Vito to express his apologies, his gratitude and whatever else might have tripped off his dangerously unguarded tongue.

She had persuaded Tim to compromise with a letter, overruling his conviction that that was the cowardly way out and tactfully hinting that it might be much less embarrassing all round if he met Vito at some time in the future when the dust on the wrecked Ferrari had at least had time to settle.

'Well, it mightn't have been precisely the way I would have chosen to meet him again...' Tim's gaze slewed guiltily away from hers as he reddened. 'But yes, it gave Vito and me a chance to talk.'

'Do you think you could end up marrying him this time?'

'It's a little too soon to say.'

Tim shook his head. 'But he must be really hung up on you to let me off...'

Ashley kept right on smiling. This was the right way to handle Tim. He was going home on study leave to swot for his A-levels. She didn't want him worrying about her. Their parents were back from New Zealand and had not a clue that they might have been faced with a far more traumatic homecoming. In fact, just about everything in everybody's garden but her own was coming up roses.

Tim kicked at the rucksack at his feet. 'When I get home, I'm going to sell my car and send the money to Vito.'

'You can't do that. Dad will want to know why!' Ashley argued in horror.

Her brother grimaced. 'I can't pay Vito back in full, but I have to do what I can.'

'Won't his insurance pay out?'

'That's not the point, is it?' Tim sighed. 'I can't forget what I did to his car. I can't act as if it isn't my responsibility just because you got me off the hook.'

'You're going to tell Dad the truth,' she guessed, dully aware of where the blame would ultimately be laid.

Leaving the station, she got on a bus that would take her to Vito's apartment. Although she had yet to actually move in, she had left her bedsit and had ferried her possessions over there early this morning before she left to spend the day with Tim. If she was clever enough, this marriage might never happen. Step one was move into the apartment rather than provoke another row with Vito. And Step two? By the time she had finished telling him about the unlikelihood of her ever producing a child in a reasonable time-frame, he might well think better of his proposition. She was hardly the ideal candidate.

The bottom line of her predicament was simple. How much was Vito powered by a desire for a son and heir, and how much by a desire for revenge? That the acquisition of a son and heir should be that important to him she didn't even question. Her own father had been unashamedly obsessed by his need for a son. On the day that Ashley had been born, another daughter instead of the son he wanted so badly, Hunt Forrester had walked out of the hospital and hadn't reappeared until it was time to take his wife and newborn child home again.

With a weary sigh she employed the key she had found lying on the antique cabinet in the hall and let herself into the apartment. Planning to make an impressive semblance of unpacking, she walked down to the smaller bedroom she had selected for herself and stopped dead on the threshold. Her cases were gone. She pulled open a wardrobe door, to be greeted by the fluttering draperies of unfamiliar garments. Opening the drawers in the chest won her the same disorientating discovery.

'Where the hell have you been?'

Ashley spun violently in shock. She had believed she was alone in the apartment. Vito was lounging in the doorway like a thunderous black cloud. Every inch of his long, lean physique spoke of electric tension. Ebony-dark eyes glittered rawly over her jean clad figure.

'I thought you were still in Geneva!'

'I've been trying to contact you here at the apartment for five days!' he delivered grimly. 'So I ask you again, where have you been? You only brought your stuff over this morning.'

Ignoring the demand for an explanation, Ashley shrugged. 'And where is my stuff?' she asked instead.

'I dumped it.'

Ashley stared at him for one long stunned moment. 'I beg your pardon?'

'Every shred of clothing you possess,' Vito confirmed. 'I dumped it all.'

Ashley moistened her dry mouth slowly. 'I don't believe you.'

He flung open the wardrobe. 'I went shopping in Geneva. You dress like a bag-lady. You needed a fresh start.'

'A b-bag-lady?' Ashley stammered, still unwilling to accept that he was telling her the truth. Although Vito had been incredibly arrogant four years ago, he would never have dared to go this far.

'In fact the only time I ever saw you out of the bag-lady guise was the night we first met. Voluminous T-shirts and loose trousers and boots—that's what you live in. For some peculiar reason, you despise your own femininity——'

'That's untrue ... ridiculous,' she protested shakily.

'I must have been blind four years ago. You hate being a woman.' Vito surveyed her with formidable calm, his earlier anger apparently cooled.

He had seen too much and too well. Ashley felt as though he had flailed off an entire layer of her skin, leaving her naked and exposed, her inner privacy compromised by his probing dissection. Her femininity had never been a cause for pride or celebration in a family where being a woman was a severe handicap.

Even in her own home, she had been a cuckoo in the nest, a lively, outspoken child with tomboyish habits, far too different from her mother and her older sister ever to fit. It had only ever been when Ashley did something wrong that her father deigned to notice her. As she moved into her teens, that wounding indifference had contributed to her increasing rebellion. Even Susan had not had it half as tough as Ashley had had. Susan had always scored points on being submissive and ladylike and—oh, yes, what was that word her father was so fond of?—womanly.

She stared bitterly into the wardrobe at the exquisite fabrics on view. 'So you've finally captured a real live doll to dress up,' she breathed painfully. 'Just remember that the fantasy woman you create will only be on the outside. Underneath it will still be me.'

Vito cleared his throat almost roughly. 'I want you to realise your potential.'

Like a good investment, she reflected, all choked up inside as she absent-mindedly tugged open a drawer. She should have expected this. It was part of the 'shape-up and conform' routine. Clothes didn't matter to her— they never had. He never had liked the way she dressed, but she still felt so incredibly hurt.

'Tell me, does the prospect of wearing silk and lace in my bed instead of a Snoopy nightshirt really embarrass you this much?'

He was trying to save face for her. He knew he had hurt her. Her teeth gritted at the awareness of what he was doing but it scared her that he should read her so accurately even after four years.

'I don't embarrass that easily.' But she did. The revealing clothes that would glorify the female body and the sensuously sinful lingerie were all so foreign and threatening to her that she shrank at the very idea of wearing them. It would be as though she was colluding with Vito, encouraging him to treat her as some brainless little sex object whose one goal in life was to please her lord and master.

'The remainder of your possessions are in there.' He indicated a box in the corner. It was full to the brim with photo albums, diaries, the really personal possessions that she would have missed.

'Who went through it all?'

'I did.'

The admission didn't bother her the way she felt it should have. Vito never pried. Vito had always respected her privacy. She had kept a diary since she was twelve and she couldn't break the habit. She had never worried that Vito couldn't be trusted in the vicinity of the written truth of her secret thoughts. Yes, she conceded dully, she had always trusted Vito not to let her down, not to betray her.

That was why she had been so savaged, so destroyed by his marriage to Carina. He had told her that he loved her, that he would always love her, that, no matter what she did, that love would always be there, and, fool that she was, she had begun to believe, she had begun to listen. It had just been words, and words were cheap. But Ashley hadn't known that when he'd walked out. She had really truly believed then that Vito loved her and that, no matter how bad things were between them, he would be back once his hot temper cooled. Instead he had married another woman, scarring Ashley so deeply with that ultimate betrayal that she didn't believe she would ever have the courage to love anyone ever again.

'If we're to make dinner before the opera, you'd better get changed.'

'Why don't you pick something for me?' she enquired acidly. 'That's what you do with a Barbie doll.'

Unconcerned by the taunt, he tossed a black evening gown on the bed like a statement. It was a gorgeous dress. The fabric was shot through with superb gold embroidery. It must have cost him a fortune.

'There's something you ought to know before you marry me,' she said abruptly.

'Last week we made an agreement.' In spite of the quiet intonation, hard determination emanated from the brilliant dark eyes raking her pale face. 'I kept my side of the deal and I have every intention of ensuring that you keep yours.'

'I won't be able to give you a child!' The pained admission was ripped from her constricted throat.

'You mean that you're not prepared to give me one.' His hard features were curiously shuttered, his tone rawedged. For a second time she was assailed by that appalling suspicion. Could he know about her previous pregnancy? She searched his flat dark eyes, found nothing there and hurriedly put her fears down to nervous paranoia. He couldn't possibly know, she told herself again.

'No, that's not what I mean. In my family——' she hesitated and then forced herself to continue '——we're not very efficient at producing children. Susan hasn't even bothered to try. My mother may have had three children but she had to go through eleven miscarriages to get them——'

'Distressing as this information is, I really don't see what it has to do with us——'

'Send me to a doctor, then!' Ashley cut in wildly. 'I bet he tells you that I'm a very poor bet!'

Vito's mouth curled with something akin to revulsion. 'You're not a brood mare, you're a woman. I wouldn't dream of sending you to a doctor. If it doesn't happen for us, it doesn't happen, but let us at least give nature a chance.'

'You won't listen to me, will you?' she whispered.

'I think you will do and say anything to escape marrying me.'

She worried at her lower lip with her teeth and looked up to find Vito's golden gaze clinging to her soft, full mouth with blatant sexual intensity. Her skin dampened betrayingly. With difficulty she dredged her eyes from his. 'And...and doesn't that bother you?'

'Not in the slightest,' he countered huskily. 'I have what *I* want.'

As the door slid quietly shut on his exit, Ashley shivered, suddenly cold. Yes, he had her in the very palm of his hand, and if she was very, very good he might be reasonable, but if she was bad, if she continued to fight, he would close that hard hand of his into a fist, because if there was one thing Vito did not excel at, it was patience.

She had a quick shower in the adjoining bathroom. Sliding into the clinging embrace of the black gown, she sat down at the dressing-table and ran a brush through her rippling swath of hair. She didn't want to look at herself. The expensive fabric skimmed and lovingly shaped the perfect curves Vito was so determined to put on show. Oddly enough, she had been wearing black the night they first met as well...

And suddenly she was back there on New Year's Eve at the start of the evening that had derailed her entire life. She had been alone and, let's face it, she thought, feeling pretty sorry for herself. All her flatmates were at home with their families but Ashley had had an appalling row with her father on Boxing Day. The next morning, wallowing in guilt at the sight of her mother's reddened eyes, she had caught the train back to London, conscious that once she was gone her father would cool down again.

One of her flatmates' friends had landed on the doorstep—Phoebe, the deb type, who was just putting in her time at university until a suitable young man popped that all-important question. She had had an invitation to a big party. Another girl had let her down and she hadn't wanted to go alone.

It was the most important party of the year, Phoebe had pleaded, and all these fabulously rich, important people would be there and her poor mother had gone to such agonising lengths to get her that invitation. Amused by her drama, Ashley had decided that it would be fun to see how the upper ten per cent of society entertained themselves. Phoebe had loaned her the proverbial little black dress and all the trimmings. And Ashley had been unwillingly fascinated by the seductive stranger she saw in the mirror.

'Gosh, you look incredibly eye-catching.' Phoebe had frowned. 'Jill would have been less competition.'

In the taxi, Phoebe had also lent her words of wisdom. 'Don't say you're a student. It sounds too brainy. Say you're a secretary or something and don't whatever you do admit your age. Teenies aren't in great demand.'

It had been a private party in a Mayfair hotel and twenty minutes into the evening Phoebe had met up with the male she had come to meet and had disappeared into the crush. Ashley had been engulfed by eager young men and several glasses of champagne later she had been reaping a vicarious thrill from all the attention she was receiving. She had had few nights out during her first term at university. Her father had kept her so short of money that she had had to work every free hour she could steal from her studies as a waitress to make ends meet.

When the tiger lily was delivered, she had been catching her breath at a table. 'That can't be for me,' she had said.

'For the lady at table twenty-two,' the waiter had insisted.

A magnum of pink champagne had arrived next. Her male companion had started to become annoyed. 'What's going on?' he had bleated. 'Is this some sort of send-up?'

'Someone's made a mistake.' She had fingered the opulent little box containing the tiger lily, dismayed to discover that something perilously close to mushy romanticism was making her resent the knowledge that the flamboyant gifts could not possibly be for her.

'What the hell do you want now?' her companion had demanded when the grinning waiter reappeared a third time. He had deposited a business card in front of her with a theatrical flourish.

'The gentleman would like you to join him, madam.'

'Is he in a wheelchair?'

'No, madam. He's seated at table three,' he had replied, deadpan.

She had glanced at the name, crunched up the card and dropped it in the ashtray, fighting the pull of her own fascination. It was her companion who had rescued the card and turned a sort of puce shade. 'Vito di Cavalieri?'

Ashley had screened a yawn. 'I've never heard of him.'

'I've never come across anyone who hasn't heard of Vito di Cavalieri.' He had looked at her as though he suspected she was a gatecrasher.

'I bet he's his own best publicist.'

His jaw had thrust out. 'He has a very bad reputation with women.'

'But what does he look like?' Little quivers of excitement had been leaping shamelessly through her veins at the style Vito had employed to introduce himself.

'Somebody else can damned well play Cupid!' he had snapped, and stormed off.

Curiosity had been eating her alive. She had sauntered up the steps from the dance-floor, striving to appear unconcerned, meaning only to steal a covert glance on

her way to the cloakroom. But the covert glance had
become a most uncool stare. While she hovered, Vito
had slid upright and strolled forward to greet her, his
raking appraisal every bit as intense as her own.

'Why didn't you just ask me to dance?' she had
mumbled, all of an adolescent quiver.

'I don't compete with a crowd.' Dark golden eyes had
enveloped her like hot, liquid honey. The high-voltage
charge of sexual awareness had been so powerful that
she had felt dizzy, disorientated and utterly detached
from her usual argumentative and unromantic self.

'And if I hadn't come up here——?'

'I was coming to get you,' he had completed softly,
and, lifting her hand, he had pressed his mouth intimately to the tender skin on the inside of her wrist and
every bone in her body had begun to melt and fuse beneath her skin.

On the one and only occasion when she had accidentally met his teenage sister, Giulia, the other girl had
demanded to know how they had met. Ashley had been
truthful. Giulia had stared at her with enormous round
eyes and flatly refused to believe her.

'You're joking, you've got to be,' Giulia had insisted.
'Vito's the most boringly conventional guy you could
meet. He never deviates from his life of workaholic duty
and devotion to the bank. He's unbelievably old-
fashioned...that's why he suits Carina down to the
ground, and when he marries her——'

Giulia had gone scarlet and hastily changed the
subject. That had been the first time she'd heard Carina's
name, but not the last. Ashley had been subtle. She had
questioned Vito ever so sneakily and had in her naïveté
learnt nothing to dismay her. Carina was virtually one
of his family, the daughter of close friends, who frequently came to stay. He had actually laughed when he'd
confided that his parents had this rather unreal hope that
he might one day decide to marry Carina. 'And pigs
might fly' had gone politely unsaid.

Why hadn't she run like a rabbit four years ago? She had recognised his maturity and sophistication. Indeed, in a foolish attempt to ease up on to a more equal level, she had spouted the secretary story and added four years to her age. Neither wit nor pride had distinguished her in Vito's company. From her early teens she had been accustomed to male interest. She had never had any trouble keeping boyfriends under control. Invariably she had had the stronger personality, and she had called every shot.

But from the first moment Vito had been the one in control, she the one struggling to hold her own in the dialogue. That humbling fact had challenged her. She had been pretty provocative once or twice, she conceded grudgingly. In addition, the champagne level had been dangerously high in her bloodstream.

He had kissed her while they were dancing. That kiss had burned all the way down to her feet and back up again. That kiss was all that it had taken to wipe out year after year of self-taught feminist conditioning.

She had drifted out into the night to be tucked into a chauffeur-driven limo and somehow within minutes she had been in his arms again, the victim of a quite agonising need for constant physical contact. She had left Phoebe's shoes behind in the lift on the way up to his apartment. She had lost her dress in the hall. Her brain— well, her brain had never made it out of the hotel, had it?

'All my life I have dreamt of meeting a woman like you,' Vito had groaned, depriving her of her first stocking one step through the bedroom door. 'And now that I have finally found you I will never let you go. So much passion...such glorious spontaneity...'

And, true to form, the passion and spontaneity he had rejoiced in the night before were unwelcome in the cold light of the following morning. For an apparently sophisticated male, Vito had been shocked rigid when he'd seen the bloodstains on the sheet. While she had been cringing with chagrin, Vito had acted more like a judge than a lover. Why hadn't she said no? How could she have let him treat her like that? Didn't she realise what a precious commodity virginity was? Why had she pretended to be something that she wasn't? And what age was she anyway? In daylight she didn't look twenty-three.

A teenager? He had gone white. Did she realise that he had a sister not very much younger? Stark naked, he had prowled about the bedroom, ranting in Italian but using just enough English to ensure that she understood the gist of his fury. And the gist of the message had been that she was so stupid in her lack of care for herself that she wasn't fit to be let out on her own. He had then, with awesome arrogance, chosen to conclude that she had been extremely lucky to meet someone like him.

Trembling with embarrassment and fury, Ashley had wrapped herself in a sheet and raced about the room picking up pieces of her clothing.

'What are you doing?' Vito had demanded.

'I'm going home.'

'But we need to talk.' He had appeared thunderstruck by her announcement.

'Is that usual after a one-night stand?' she had asked bitterly.

'That is not what it was!' Vito had raked back at her fiercely. 'I've never had a one-night stand in my life. *Dio*, what sort of a man do you think I am? Last night was about a great deal more than sex.'

'You could have fooled me.'

'How did you expect me to react today? You lied to me,' he had condemned. 'If I'd known you were a virgin, I'd never have slept with you. I must have been insane. I didn't even take precautions when we made love. I have never been so irresponsible. You could be pregnant...'

Ashley had allowed a glittering little smile to touch her ripe mouth, repayment for the mortification she had been forced to endure. 'Oh, I don't think so. I'm on the Pill.'

'But you were a——'

'So?' She had watched his darkly handsome face harden as he drew the conclusion she had intended: that she had been ready for a lover and she had simply chosen him. In fact she had been put on the Pill to correct irregularities in her menstrual cycle, and protection from possible pregnancy had been the last thing on her mind.

The curtains fell on the past, plunging her back to the present. She reflected sadly that that was where her proud pretence had begun. The very first day. She had refused to let Vito see her confusion and vulnerability. All she had wanted to do was escape. She had been furious with herself, furious with him but she had also known that what had happened to them both the previous night had been mutual, something incredibly powerful and special that she just couldn't bear to walk away from, something she had honestly never dreamt she could feel with any man. But to be frank, she allowed reluctantly, those feelings had frightened the hell out of her.

'Are you ready?'

She stood up slowly, desperate uncertainty and self-consciousness etched into her every movement. Tall, dark and extravagantly gorgeous in a dinner jacket, Vito audibly caught his breath. 'You look like a pre-Raphaelite painting.'

'And I feel like a bimbo.'

His sensual mouth twisted wryly. 'I wouldn't worry. The minute you open your mouth, any resemblance vanishes.'

In the car, she said, 'Your family won't accept me. Four years ago, they thought I was just some cheap little waitress you were slumming with!'

His gaze whipped over sharply. 'Exactly how do you know that they might think of you like that?'

In the heat of the moment she had been incautious but she was not prepared to tell him about his mother's visit. That would be too, too degrading. Not that Elena di Cavalieri had been rude or crude. Vito's mother had been far too much of a lady to behave like that. No, what had hurt the most had been Elena's visible desperation as she sought to persuade Ashley that she would ruin Vito's life if she married him. In fact, Elena had come pitifully close to begging. It might almost have been funny if it hadn't been so horribly humiliating.

'Ashley, I asked you a question.'

'I guessed how your family would think about me.'

His dark eyes were nailed to her shuttered face. 'And did that influence your response to my proposal of marriage?'

Proposal? She held on to a howl of contemptuous laughter at that so flattering euphemism. Other women got soft lights and flowers. What had she got? Vito had not got down on bended knee or anything like that. She didn't quite recall how he had opened the subject, but she did recall being blistered with the reminder that she had been sharing his bed for five months and that she was damned lucky he didn't value her quite as cheaply as she valued herself. Her morals were not his, he had asserted. Women willing to share his bed were two a penny. What he wanted was a wife and future mother of his children.

'Ashley,' he prompted tautly.

'It didn't influence me. I didn't want to marry you.' But Ashley was grimly aware that that was not quite the whole truth. Two days after finding out about the baby, she had phoned Vito in Italy. Giulia had taken the call and she had told Ashley with audible embarrassment that Vito was in the middle of his engagement party and did she still want to speak to him? Ashley had replaced the receiver without replying, so shocked and incredulous that she hadn't been able to think of a single face-saving thing to say. It was absolutely impossible to guess now what might have happened between them had Vito not turned with such indecent haste to another woman.

'But *this* time you will marry me.' Vito's bone-structure stood out starkly beneath his golden skin. His eyes splintered into hers in raw challenge. 'And very possibly you won't be so smug and self-satisfied when that marriage comes to an end.'

'I'm not smug about it!' Ashley argued with real vehemence.

Vito slung her a simmering glance of complete contempt. 'I'm going to chip you out of that aggressive little shell you live in, piece by piece. I'm going to strip off every layer you hide behind until there's nowhere left to run!'

'If you do that I'll hate you even more than I do now!' Dry-mouthed, Ashley stared back at him, paralysed by the terrifying amount of threat he could emanate.

'So what have I got to lose?' he gritted.

They dined at Nico at Ninety on Park Lane. A powerful ripple of interest, both discreet and otherwise, accompanied their entrance. Her pale skin flaming, Ashley dug her head into her menu and was confronted by a view of her own cleavage that made her feel even more hatefully self-conscious. She ordered her own meal. Vito didn't bat an eyelash. The veal braised in Madeira melted in her mouth and her tension began to mellow, her shoulders to straighten. As she rested back in her chair to sip at her wine, she thrust the heavy fall of her hair irritably back behind one small ear, exposing the slender length of her neck.

'Some day I shall have it all cut off,' she said, absently expecting him to argue at the very idea and inwardly acknowledging that her hair was her one claim to vanity. But silence greeted her and she tilted her head back to look at him.

Vito was staring fixedly at her, and what she saw in his hard features shocked her rigid. Eyes as cold and treacherous as black ice were nailed to her. Perspiration broke out on her brow. 'What's wrong?' she demanded. 'Why are you looking at me like that?'

Vito tossed his napkin down beside the plate he had thrust away, his meal apparently abandoned. 'I believe it's time we returned to a subject I allowed you to ignore earlier,' he breathed very, very quietly. 'Where were you today?'

She frowned in bewilderment. 'I spent the day with Tim. He's leaving London to go home and swot for his exams.'

The flash of pure naked rage that illuminated Vito's dark gaze to piercing brilliance made her flinch. For a split-second she honestly believed that if a table hadn't separated them Vito would have clenched the brown fingers flexing on the arm of his chair round her throat instead. Her throat, yes, for, strange as it might seem, Vito was not directly meeting her eyes for longer than a second at a time. His smouldering gaze continually dropped below the level of her chin.

He drew in a deep, shuddering breath. Even the naturally olive tone of his complexion couldn't hide the fact that he was literally white with the kind of rage that visibly threatened even his intimidating self-discipline. 'You're lying,' he murmured with raw menace. 'This morning, when I found your cases in the apartment, I telephoned your sister to see if you were with her. She told me that your brother had caught the train home a few hours earlier...'

Ashley instantly understood that Tim had told a white lie to her sister sooner than risk offending Susan with the news that he intended to spend his last day with Ashley, rather than her. 'He only pretended to be catching an early train. We spent the day together and——'

Vito elevated an ebony brow. 'Then no doubt he gave you that bite on your neck,' he incised in a bitterly derisive undertone.

'Bite?' she repeated, her hand flying up to her throat instinctively to feel the small tender spot just below her right ear. Was there a bruise there? Dimly she recalled stretching unwarily across an opened suitcase to pull something out from behind the lid. The protruding lock had caught her a painful blow which she had massaged and as quickly forgotten while she got on with her packing.

'You little slut...' Vito slashed back at her in a murderous undertone that chilled her blood in her veins and sent her heartbeat thudding in a race to the foot of her constricting throat. 'You filthy little slut. You spent the day being bedded by your lover...'

'Th-that's a lie,' Ashley stammered, so shattered by his unjust and ridiculous accusation that she could think of nothing more original to say in the confining spaces of a public place.

'And if I hadn't seen the evidence, I'd never have known,' Vito growled, lashing himself into a fury made all the more powerful by the suffocating constraints of their situation. He signalled for the bill. Dousing the waiter's anxiety that there had been something wrong with the meal, he waved him away again, to her disbelief. 'We'll finish our wine,' he said between gritted even white teeth.

'Vito, please... let's get out of here,' she whispered.

Lounging back into his chair, he emitted a humourless laugh that bounced off her raw nerve-endings like a brick shattering glass. He threw back his darkly handsome head, seething golden eyes striking hers in unconcerned challenge. 'No,' he said very softly. 'You're going to listen, and here you are at least safe. Outside, the way I feel right now, you'd be in considerable danger. I'm not sure I could keep my hands off you, because I really don't see why I should——'

'Vito——' she pleaded, sitting still as a graven image, mesmerised by a great spreading nameless terror of she knew not what. It was the way he was looking at her. She had seen Vito angry countless times but she had never seen him as angry as this... as though he could wipe her off the face of the earth without a moment's regret.

'You see, I've been far too soft with you. I always was. This evening you accused me of trying to create my fantasy woman,' he reminded her with a scornful twist to his grim mouth. 'I should have laughed like a hyena.

Whatever you are to me, you are not and never could be my fantasy. That would require a miracle. I didn't intend to broach this subject now, but since you have chosen to remind me in the crudest possible way of what you are, I really can't let this moment go past——'

'I don't know what you're talking about,' she murmured tightly.

'But all over again you have just proved what you are,' Vito condemned with the ice that was already starting to close in the anger and that freezing calm was all the more deadly a weapon in his possession. 'Four years ago you moved out of my apartment within twenty-four hours of my departure. And where did you go?'

The oxygen she needed to breathe was being squeezed out of her lungs by a giant invisible hand.

He watched the last scrap of colour slide from her cheeks. 'You didn't go back to the room in the dingy flat, did you? The room you insisted on holding on to throughout our entire relationship. So, where did you go? You leapt straight into bed with another man——'

'No!' she gasped, and as heads turned at a nearby table she bit her tongue and closed her eyes, fighting for self-control.

'He wasn't a man, though, was he? He was just a kid,' Vito continued in the same murderously quiet voice that now betrayed absolutely no emotion.

'He was just a friend,' she whispered in anguish.

'So you like to screw your friends as well,' Vito flicked back with chilling brutality. 'You moved in with him. From my bed to his bed within hours. Now how would you describe a woman who behaves like that?'

'You've got it wrong——' she began.

'No,' Vito contradicted with succinct emphasis. 'I would very much prefer to have it wrong, because the unlovely truth did nothing for my ego, but that sensation of entirely superficial hurt male pride was very swiftly to be replaced by something far more meaningful and far more powerful...'

He let the assurance hang there and she started to tremble, assailed by a premonition of disaster so strong that she was engulfed by it, silently waiting for the axe to fall.

'Yes,' Vito breathed flatly. 'A month after you moved in with him you kept an appointment at an abortion clinic to take care of the little problem that had so inconveniently arisen. And you didn't exactly kill that little problem with kindness, did you?'

A great sob was rising in her throat like the wail of a trapped animal in agony. She bowed her head, unable to speak. If she had opened her mouth she would have broken down and utterly disgraced herself. She was in a state of such complete shock that she couldn't even think, and later she would not remember leaving the restaurant where Vito had chosen cruelly to rip away that last veil of privacy.

CHAPTER FIVE

ASHLEY was traumatised. She sat in the back of the limo like a zombie. Vito had hit her with the one condemnation against which she felt she had no defence. Indeed, she almost felt as though she deserved his revulsion. How he knew didn't matter. It was simply that he did know. It seemed pointless to explain that she had moved into Steve's flat because she had had nowhere else to go. She had sublet her room shortly before she broke up with Vito in an effort to cut down her expenses.

Steve had let her sleep on the sofa. He had been a good friend, supporting her when she'd most needed support but too young and immature even to begin to understand the complexity of a woman's feelings when she realised that she was pregnant and she didn't want to be.

Ashley's first reaction had been sheer terror, and when she had learnt that Vito was getting engaged to Carina she had gone to pieces. She had been petrified of what her father would do if he found out. Steve had made the first appointment for her. He had pointed out that Vito was gone, that she was on her own, and furthermore that she had never wanted children. A termination was the only practical solution, he had said. She didn't have the money to keep a baby. How was she going to live? What sort of a life was she going to give the baby?

She had gone for counselling but it hadn't penetrated. She had felt ill and weak and wretched and desperately alone in spite of Steve's efforts to the contrary. And, when the day scheduled for the termination had arrived, she had gone. But ten minutes through the door her pregnancy had suddenly and for the very first time become painfully real to her. She had started to wonder whether the baby was a boy or a girl and whether it would have red hair or black hair or green eyes or dark eyes, and she had begun, slowly and agonisingly, to come apart at the seams as she finally faced up to the fact that practicality and pregnancy were two very uneasy partners.

When she had finally admitted that she just couldn't go through with it, she had been in such an emotional state that the staff had insisted they let her contact someone to come and collect her. She had given them Susan's telephone number because Steve had had an exam that day. And that was how she had come to tell Susan something that she would never have told her had she been more in control.

She had told Susan that, no matter how hard it was, she intended to have her baby and keep it. And she had meant it, every word of it. Indeed it was that announcement which had nearly driven her father to violence. When she had miscarried she had felt as though it was some heavenly punishment, a judgement on her for not wanting her baby from the beginning. Her intelligence told her that was nonsense, but the feeling of immense guilt had somehow survived.

'Vito...' she muttered.

'The subject is closed.'

'Then why did you open it?' Ashley was distraught, wholly at the mercy of emotion and reaction, with no space left for considered thought.

His hard profile was unyielding. 'I don't like secrets. I should have faced you with it the first day.'

'I didn't have an abortion...I miscarried,' she whispered painfully.

'Your one great gift used to be the ability to tell the truth no matter how unwelcome it was! Don't insult my intelligence.'

'I never slept with Steve in my life!' Although something in the back of her mind was telling her to shut up, she just had to defend herself.

'Figuratively speaking, you may well be telling the truth,' Vito conceded with cutting bite. 'You didn't sleep very much in my bed either.'

He was inviolable, immovable, his beliefs set in stone. Yet, deprived of her usual mainstay of anger by the sheer depth of her inner pain, she still persisted. 'I was with Tim today,' she told him again. 'And that bruise happened when I bent over a suitcase this morning and collided with the lock. Furthermore, I haven't got a lover.'

'You have sex with your partners. Love would indeed be a euphemism.'

He actually took her to the opera. She couldn't believe that he could be that cruel but he was. And Ashley, who had always loved the opera, heard nothing but a deafening cacophony of soaring voices coming at her from all sides in their private box. He hadn't listened. He hadn't given her protestations even a fleeting hearing. He didn't believe her, he was never going to believe her and she had no proof to offer in her own defence. The tears coursed soundlessly down her drawn cheeks.

He took her back to the apartment before the intermission. The silence between them was like a great glass wall and she was too drained to try and climb it. She vanished into her bedroom without a word and tore off the finery he had chosen to frame her in before he smashed her down. She had never been so hurt that she physically ached, but she did now as she crawled naked into the bed like a wounded animal seeking sanctuary. She heard the thud of the front door shutting on his departure and then the dam burst again. He had brought it all back, opening up scars that had yet to heal.

'Ashley, please...' She was startled into a scream when a hand brushed aside the tangle of hair concealing the face she had buried in the pillow to muffle her sobs.

'Go a-away!' she sobbed.

The mattress gave under the onslaught of his weight. 'I was callous and sadistic. I was a total bastard. I admit it. I wanted to hurt you——'

'You did,' she gasped. 'Now go away and let me do my grieving in private.'

'In all the time we were together four years ago, I never once saw you cry. And now twice in a week...' His roughened voice broke off. 'You were always so tough——'

'I used to cry in the b-bathroom with the shower running.'

Vito loosed a laugh utterly devoid of humour. 'I wish I'd known.'

'You would have revelled in it,' she mumbled, and sat up, scrunching the sheet defensively round her and concealing her swollen face below the veil of her tousled hair. 'I thought you'd gone...'

'I couldn't leave you like this. I came back.' He slotted a brandy into her hand and she drank it down like a Cossack about to go into battle. The alcohol eased the ache in her throat but she still refused to look at him.

He laced long fingers into her hair and tipped up her face, preventing her retreat. 'We're getting married in ten days' time and then I have a six-week vacation, which we will spend in Sri Lanka.'

She trembled at the implacability she met in his fierce dark eyes. Other emotions were beginning to surface from beneath the crushing weight of feeling she had given vent to. No wonder he had called her a whore that first day in his office. Only a woman worthy of that name would have behaved as he believed she had four years ago and again today. He had talked about abortion as though she were so without female sensitivity that such a choice would have meant absolutely nothing to her. Hatred surged in a hot, reviving rush through the cracks he had made in her composure. Loathing at his injustice began to crackle in a series of little fires fed by bitter resentment.

He had married another woman, yet he reserved the right to stand in judgement over her for almost making a choice that many women would have made in her position. The guilt she had long borne burnt out forever in that moment. The urge to clear her name that had weakened her response to his bitter prejudice earlier vanished entirely. He hadn't even asked if the child was his. Presumably he thought she couldn't possibly know whether it had been or not. So now she had it all. The truth as Vito saw it, and the motivation behind his coercion.

If he had not loved her, he had certainly been physically obsessed by her. Unsuitable as she was, he had stayed with her five months and he had asked her to marry him. The sensation of what he had termed an 'entirely superficial hurt' to his male pride had been a masterful understatement which appearances could no longer sustain. Her refusal to marry him four years ago must have absolutely devastated him, and the belief that she had immediately turned to another man had added an entire chapter to that devastation. The savagery with which he had condemned her had been revealing. Carina clearly hadn't managed to soothe that rawness. Evidently only the most bitter of revenge scenarios was capable of taking away that slur on his manhood.

'Is it possible for us to start again?' The abrasive demand was literally wrenched from him as he stared down at her, a tiny pulse pulling at the taut edge of his wide mouth. 'This is not how I meant it to be.'

'Blood and gore every five minutes? Why don't you just arrange for me to have an accident?' Ashley enquired shakily. 'It would be so much quicker and cleaner.'

The long brown fingers knotted into the fiery strands of her hair. The ferocity of his brilliant gaze stabbed into her like a knife. 'Hate and love are but two sides of the same coin.'

'You'd better watch out, then. This much hate comes uncomfortably close to manic obsession,' she muttered, her breath tripping in her dry throat.

'And you should know why,' Vito traded, his fingers tightening with the raw tension that smouldered from him.

In his grip, she gave a tiny compulsive shudder, suddenly becoming alarmingly aware of the intimacy of their surroundings combined with her nudity and his white-hot sexual temperament. The vibrations in the atmosphere were shooting round her like invisible lightning bolts, making it incredibly hard for her to breathe. 'Because I said no? Because I had the incredible bad taste to find another man?' she threw at him in provocative intent, hoping to douse the dark flames of arousal in his intent stare.

Vito didn't even flinch. True, a momentary gravity tightened his facial muscles, but the idea that she had so swiftly sought consolation was evidently so ingrained that she could not shock him. 'Because I loved you,' he grated, and she was the one most inconveniently shocked by that confession. 'You look surprised, but why should you? Do you really believe that lust rejected would still incite me to such violence?' He ran the fingertips of his other hand up along the line of her extended throat in a caressing gesture that was curiously chilling. 'Love? I believed it couldn't happen to me. I had given up all hope of it ever happening. I was twenty-eight years old and, in many ways, older than my years. And then one night I saw you on a dance-floor and I wanted you more than anything I had ever wanted in my life...'

Ashley was trembling, curiously unwilling to accept the truth of what she had once believed. 'Infatuation,' she said fiercely. 'And it burnt out for both of us.'

'But this didn't...' One forceful hand welding to her taut spine, Vito lowered his dark head. His breath fanned her cheek and then he let his teeth nip playfully at the soft fullness of her lower lip, soothing the tiny assault with the teasing tip of his tongue until involuntarily her mouth opened, inviting a deeper invasion.

The hard heat of his body against hers was a powerful enticement. Tiny little quivers of sexual tension were awakening at every pressure-point where his lean muscles were in contact with her softer curves. Ashley began to shake, struggling to deny and to fight the insidious weakness stealing through her limbs. She could stop this, she *would* stop this, the little voice in her head screamed. He could not force her into intimacy. But a curious weighted stasis was holding her still in his embrace as though she was waiting for a hurricane warning before she could actually act in her own defence.

'No...no, not this!' Her voice was hoarse with the effort it took to break the spell.

He clenched both her hands in his and held her back from him before she could take a single evasive movement. His intent gaze smouldered over her. As she glanced down at herself, she saw the revealing thrust of her nipples against the fine percale sheet still draped across her breasts, and her translucent skin burned with the heat of her own betrayal.

A dark flush accentuated the harsh set of his features. 'If you can't live without a man, that man might as well be me,' he grated roughly.

Fury speared through that all-pervasive physical frailty. Between clenched teeth, she spat, 'If rape turns you on, go ahead!'

A glimmer of black humour softened the hard set of his sensual mouth. 'How you do love to dramatise yourself. Why can't you be honest about this at least? You saw me for the first time in four and a half years last week and within minutes you were hot all over, eating me with your eyes——'

Outraged, Ashley shrieked, 'That's a filthy lie!'

Vito dealt her a flashing smile of all-male satisfaction. 'Console yourself with the thought that if you hadn't looked at me like that, you wouldn't be here now. You dug your own grave, *cara*.'

With a superhuman effort Ashley took advantage of his loosened hold and, dragging her hands free, leapt off the bed. Snatching up the dress she had earlier discarded, she fled the room. The rest of the apartment was unhelpfully in darkness and she skidded in the direction of the hall, uncertain of her bearings.

Vito caught her hand and in her determination to escape she tore her fingers free so violently that she fell back against the wall. 'You're out of control!' she gasped strickenly as he trapped her there, one hand squarely planted on either side of her head in the depths of her hair.

'And so are you,' he breathed unsteadily. 'Exactly the way I like you.'

Scarcely able to believe that this was happening to her, Ashley attempted to raise her knee, but a hard thigh pinned the recalcitrant limb in place and simultaneously Vito brought his mouth crashing down on hers.

It was like a naked flame thrown on tinder-dry straw: a complete and uncontrollable conflagration. As his tongue hungrily probed the moist recesses of her mouth, a hoarse moan of pleasure was forced from her. Her taut body went into meltdown; between one moment and the next all rational thought ceased as though he had thrown a switch. She braced her hands on his shoulders and answered that kiss with complete abandon.

Time had no meaning. All that existed was a fierce world of almost unbearable sensation which wiped out everything else. He was lifting her up to his level, burying his face in the ripe swell of her aching breasts until he found a taut nipple to tease with his mouth and feelings, physical feelings that had been held in too tight for too long suddenly exploded in a fiery gush of response. Her fingers dug into the springy depths of his black hair and she wanted to scream with the power of what she was experiencing.

Vito choked out a curse as he cannoned off a door and then he found her mouth again, feeding her desire with the overwhelming force of his own. He didn't break that contact for a second as he brought her down heavily on a bed somewhere in the darkness.

He was struggling out of his shirt and the assistance he got was negligible as her hands wandered in a helpless need for reacquaintance over the broad expanse of his chest, fingertips skating through the dark whorls of hair and down to the smoother skin at his lean waist. He felt hot, as if he was burning up, but the same flames were in her and she was lost, irretrievably lost in the scent and the feel and the touch of him.

Abruptly he wrenched back from her and ripped off the remainder of his clothes. He muttered something in Italian and then he groaned, 'How the hell do you do this to me? It wasn't supposed to be like this...'

Cooler air briefly washed her damp skin and for a split-second a shard of reason almost returned, but, before the nebulous thought could form, Vito was back in her arms with a vengeance. She gasped as long fingers slid between her thighs and found the moist centre of her desire, cried out and arched her back beneath the hot onslaught of his mouth on her taut breasts.

'Tell me how you feel,' he demanded between clenched teeth as he moved over her, his hands rough on her thighs, his body a heavy but blessed weight on hers.

'Vito, please...oh, God, please...don't stop.' She was at fever pitch, her entire being concentrated on a razor-edge of unbearable need. She could feel him, hot and hard and ready, and she couldn't wait, was terrified he might make her wait, because if he didn't drive her over that edge she thought she might die from frustration.

He took her like an invading army, ruthless in conquest. The sheer power of his first thrust forced a cry of pain from her dry lips but pain became intolerable pleasure within seconds. Her hips writhed beneath his as he drove into her in long shuddering strokes, his skin slippery with perspiration against hers. She moved to the heated rhythm he set, abandoned and driven by the most intense excitement of all, and then suddenly every muscle clenched and she was moaning with the ecstasy of fulfilment, rawly erotic shock waves spreading out from the very centre of her body to drain her momentarily of all thought and all movement. With a groan of raw satisfaction Vito subsided on her, spent and satiated. Instinctively she wrapped her arms round him and almost instantly drifted off to sleep.

When she surfaced, it was like waking up to a living hell. Lights were on, harsh and glaring, and the first things she saw when she opened her eyes were the photographs on the cabinet by the bed. Carina, smiling from a silver frame. And Carina in Vito's arms, punch-drunk with happiness in one of those informal but intimate studies that just might have been taken on a honeymoon. Ashley's stomach twisted and turned over sickly as if she had gone down too fast in a lift. She turned away and met Vito's shuttered dark gaze.

Almost fully dressed, he was shrugging a broad shoulder into the jacket of a navy pinstripe suit. He looked heartbreakingly handsome and soul-destroyingly remote. If he was feeling anything, he wasn't showing it, and that ability of his to shut everything out tortured her at a moment when she felt sick with self-hatred and humiliation. Trembling all over, she shut her eyes, struggling fiercely against her mind's determination to replay the last few hours. It would happen soon enough: the self-examination, the questions that had no welcome answers. But not now, the little voice in her head pleaded, not now... *in front of him*.

'I think I should leave.' There was no emotion whatsoever in the announcement, except that some sixth sense told her that Vito couldn't wait to get away.

She pressed her cheek into the pillow. 'Can I leave too?' she whispered, and it sounded as if she was begging, and for the first time in her life she really didn't care.

'It was inevitable that this would happen.'

'You made it happen,' she condemned.

'We made it happen,' he countered harshly. 'I didn't plan it. I intended to wait until after the wedding.'

A near-hysterical laugh escaped her and she bit down so hard on her tongue that it bled. She never had been able to cope with Vito when he froze, and he wasn't about to let her go. Vito's ancestors had been loan-sharks since the Middle Ages. Something for nothing was not a concept that had figured largely in his upbringing. Vito would take what he wanted from her regardless of the cost. He would pick her apart as he had done over dinner and then fall like a vulture on the pitiful remnants that remained. He had done it twice already and the poisonous taste of defeat was smashing her into pieces.

'You should run a little account book, stamp each page every time I——'

'Don't!' he raked at her with sudden rawness. 'It wasn't planned!'

'No?' She cast him a fleeting look because she just couldn't bring herself to face a head-on collision. 'Over dinner you smash me up. Then you trail me to the opera. Then you trail me out of the opera. Then you offer me brandy and a little bit of sympathy and then you ... and then you ... you——'

'Do you think I'm proud of what I did tonight? Do you think I'm proud that I can't keep my hands off you?' The ice had cracked. Tense as a jungle cat about to spring, he flung the demands at her with lancing ferocity.

'Why don't you throw some money on the bed?' Ashley whispered strickenly. 'Isn't that what you do with whores?'

'You are not a whore!'

'You said I was,' she persisted stubbornly.

Vito flung up both hands in a gesture of raging frustration. '*Dio,* I was jealous, so jealous that I wouldn't listen to reason. I accept now that you were with Tim today and that that stupid bruise wasn't what I assumed it was, but at the time I believed you'd been with another man!'

'And now that reason has returned I've been upgraded, have I? Well, I've got news for you,' she bit out shakily. 'I feel like a whore. How you feel has got nothing to do with how I feel.'

He swore, long and low in his own language, both hands clenched into fists. He swung round in a graceful arc and surveyed her with sudden piercing intuition. 'You think that if you make me feel bad enough I'll let you go. I won't,' he said succinctly. 'Next week we are getting married and nothing will change that fact.'

'I think the punishment exceeds the crime.'

For an instant he lingered by the door, brilliant dark eyes appraising her incredibly beautiful face. His expressive mouth tightened as though the view disturbed him. 'But whose is the punishment and whose was the crime?' he breathed tautly.

She slumped back on the bed, caught an accidental glimpse of the photographs and abruptly reared up again. Lifting them, she yanked open the cabinet drawer and dropped them inside. Now why had she done that? She didn't want to think about why. Was she jealous? Four years ago she had been so jealous—she had burnt on a rack of her own making, imagining him with her . . . over and over again.

And now here she was back in Vito's bed once more, involved in a relationship of such tortuous complexity and bitterness that she could hardly cope with her own turmoil. Somehow it was no consolation to know that Vito's incredibly disciplined intellect was very evidently suffering from a little chaos too. He hadn't planned this. No, well, ungenerous as she felt towards him, she really didn't think that he had. Vito didn't like messy situations. Vito didn't like to lose control.

And Ashley didn't like to lose control either. Passion had surged in beneath her shaky defences and had betrayed her as never before. With Vito, it had always been like that, but in the past it had been a weakness made bearable by love. Only she didn't love him any more. She had taught herself not to love him. Month after month, day in, day out, she had reminded herself of his betrayal until bitterness became her strength and hatred her armour. But what had happened to the bitterness and the hatred when she needed them most?

Had she been able to withstand that passion and remain cold, she would be free as the wind right now! Vito was far too male to feel any desire to force his attentions on an unwilling woman. She hadn't been unwilling. Her teeth gritted together in self-disgust. She had ached for the heated caress of his hands and the hot invasion of his body. It had been as if every moment, from that first meeting in his office, had been building up into exactly this climax. In the aftermath she felt sick, mortified by her own abandonment. She had wanted him...oh, yes, she had wanted him every bit as much as he appeared to want her, and consequences be damned. And why was that? She hated him, didn't she? She hated him for what he had done in the past and for what he was doing to her now.

But it didn't seem to make any difference once he touched her. She had been upset, she reminded herself frantically, deeply upset. He had caught her at the worst possible moment and somehow...somehow, she reasoned lamely, all those painful emotions had exploded into passion. A passion she had been unable to experience with anyone else. She thought of the dates she had forced herself to accept when she had so desperately wanted to feel something, anything so that she could reassure herself that she was still in the land of the living.

In fact just last year she had met one really special man. A doctor, a single parent with a little girl at the nursery. And she had really liked Josh and he had more than liked her, but when it came to crunch-time she had had to stop seeing him, because liking had flatly refused to turn into love or even desire.

And then Vito had come along and she was like a woman with a death wish. Tonight—well, tonight she had gone off the deep end. She had thought of nothing, not even consequences. And it had been years since she was on the Pill, that low-dosage Pill that had been insufficient to prevent her pregnancy. Just suppose she was like her mother, who had once joked that she could get pregnant just looking into a pram? No, it wouldn't happen, she couldn't believe it could happen to her a second time, but she didn't intend to take the risk. Tomorrow she would see a doctor and ask for a prescription for a contraceptive Pill. That would frustrate

Vito's plans for the future, and it wasn't as if he could ever find out why she was failing to become pregnant. She would be very discreet.

'I just don't think it's fair to spring this on me. I don't want to meet your family. I want nothing to do with them and I don't see why they should want anything to do with me!' Ashley vented her nervous tension in a staccato burst.

'Don't be ridiculous,' Vito parried with grating impatience, since the argument had been batting back and forth all the way through an endless traffic jam. 'Naturally they would like to meet you before the wedding.'

Her nails dug into the soft palm of one clenched hand. She didn't want to be served up like a particularly nasty surprise to Elena di Cavalieri, who probably hadn't gone to bed dry-eyed for a single night since her son had shattered her with the bombshell of his marital plans. And she most certainly didn't want another cheque pressed into her supposedly hot and grasping little hand.

'This party was my mother's idea. Why should you be hostile to the fact that she wants to welcome you into the family and introduce you to some of our friends? I can assure you that organising such a large party at such short notice was no easy matter.'

So why was she taking the trouble? Ashley thought of that tiny, stunningly lovely woman, whose apparent fragility concealed a temperament as tough as old boots. She still cringed when she thought of their last meeting. Fifteen minutes of being cut to ribbons by deep sincerity, tear-filled eyes and the inexplicable sensation that she was somehow unclean.

'I won't have her upset,' Vito said softly.

Ashley swallowed hard and smoothed the silk of her hand-painted evening gown. She was unable to avoid the flashing brilliance of the diamond ring lodged like a manacle on her wedding finger. Vito had passed it across the table over dinner last night. No frills there, she conceded, and dimly wondered what had happened to the romantic male who had once regularly presented her with flowers and little gifts with all the charm of a very Italian lover. And she hadn't wanted them, although she had struggled to appreciate the sentiment behind his need to continually give her things.

She had hated the flowers. When her father had been particularly nasty to her mother, he would always bring flowers home the next day. And her silly mother would go into ecstasies, as if some extraordinary effort had been involved in their purchase. For the very first time it occurred to her that her whole relationship with Vito four years ago had been dominated by her inner terror of somehow ending up like her mother. A tiny frown pleated her fine brows. She had never seen that before and yet it was so obvious. Her unhappy childhood had soared like a huge wall between them.

'It's not too late to invite your family to the wedding.'

Ashley shuddered. 'No, thanks.'

'Surely your sister——?'

'We're not close.'

'Have you ever let anyone close?' Vito asked with dark emphasis.

He had come closer than anyone, but he hadn't been satisfied with what she was prepared to give. It was all or nothing with Vito. If you didn't surrender everything, he thought he was being short-changed. Once a banker, always a banker. He had wanted all the accounts out on the table, all balanced and shipshape. He had not listened to the truths he desired to hear. He had simply demanded that she mould herself into the woman he wanted.

He had ignored her needs. The idea of her wanting any form of independence had been an insult to his masculinity. She had been a free spirit for the first time in her life and he had tried to cage her. And even if she had felt differently, she had been far too young for marriage and children and all the many responsibilities that both would have demanded of her. Yet Vito had thought he was offering her paradise on a plate. At least this time he knew the score, she reflected tautly.

The past week had been a period of agonising tension. Vito had taken her out three times to dinner and once to a nightclub where he didn't even ask her to dance. He had withdrawn behind a cold front as menacing as a polar freeze. Every night he had dropped her back to the apartment and left her there in solitary confinement. He hadn't laid a finger on her, and she couldn't decide whether that was supposed to be her punishment or his own. Was it any comfort to know that he had clearly found that episode of abandoned sex as devastating as she had? Did what she made him feel threaten him? It was an interesting thought.

Every light in the huge house seemed to be shining with blinding brilliance. This would be her home when they were in London, but not for very long, she told herself. She gave their marriage a year at most. When she proved to be unrewardingly infertile, by virtue of the contraception she was secretly taking, Vito would have no reason to continue the farce. And by then surely even he would have had an overdose of revenge?

A tiny figure clad in something floaty and silvery swam up to them. Ashley's nerveless hands were instantly gripped in an evident rush of warm and welcoming affection. 'I can't tell you how much I've been dying to meet you.' Elena di Cavalieri's use of English had been honed to perfection by years at an English boarding-school.

Linking a deft arm in hers, Ashley found herself carried off. Startled, she glanced back at Vito. He smiled, possibly the most genuine smile he had given her in the last fortnight, and her mouth ran dry at the sheer magnetism of that smile until she reminded herself that it was for his mother, who was clearly far too clever to show her real feelings in a no-win situation.

'I think we need to talk.' Elena pressed open a door almost furtively and all but dragged her in.

Freed, Ashley hovered in what was a most handsome library. Her future mother-in-law offered her a glass of champagne from a silver tray. The ambush had been pre-planned and there was something just a tinge desperate in Elena's very bright smile. 'Won't you sit down?'

Ashley sank down stiff-backed on an armchair, her defensive antennae prickling with wariness. 'We're getting married the day after tomorrow.' The announcement, ludicrously unnecessary in the circumstances, just flew off her unguarded tongue. She reddened fiercely, abstractedly aware that she had sounded like a woman ready to fight off all threats to the contrary.

'And nothing could make me happier,' Elena assured her levelly.

Ashley stared at her in bewilderment.

Elena sighed. 'I do mean that sincerely. I'm so desperately sorry that I interfered in what was none of my business four years ago. I made a dreadful error of judgement for all the wrong reasons and if I hadn't been so stubborn I would have told him what I had done the minute he came back from London. He was so shattered when you turned him down. I'd never seen him like that before but I told myself he'd get over it.'

'He did, but you don't need to feel responsible. I . . . I had other reasons for not marrying him,' Ashley responded uncertainly.

'Why haven't you told him about my visit?'

'There was no reason to tell him. That's in the past,' Ashley said, wanting to show that she could be equally generous.

'I really do want you to be happy with my son. I just wish that I could turn the clock back for both of you.' Elena looked a little tearful. 'And some day I hope we can become friends.'

Her sincerity was unquestionable. Elena clearly believed that she was the woman Vito loved. Ashley had been softened by her honesty and her careful avoidance of any mention of Carina but she was in no position to respond in kind. How would Elena feel when this marriage also came to an unhappy end? Ashley found herself hoping Vito's mother wouldn't start thinking that her past interference had had any bearing on that development.

Vito was standing across the hall in a clump of other men. As she approached, he immediately excused himself. Interpreting her greater relaxation, he murmured, 'I could have told you there was nothing to worry about. My mother's a very gentle woman.'

Men were so stupid sometimes, Ashley thought irritably. Elena was an unashamedly emotional woman and a ruthlessly protective mother, far less fragile than appearances might suggest. Momentarily she surprised herself with the awareness that she would rather have welcomed Elena as a friend. As it was, she wouldn't be around long enough to scratch the surface even as a daughter-in-law.

The next hour was a blur of names and faces. Vito infuriated her. The reserve she had endured all week was blatantly cast aside. He was showing her off like a trophy. Mine, that firm hand on her shoulder said. Look but don't touch, said his eyes. Self-satisfaction emanated from him in waves. Only one of his three sisters was present. Giulia, proudly pregnant in a beautiful designer gown, greeted her like an old friend.

'I'm so happy for you and Vito,' she said warmly. 'I insisted on being here tonight. I wouldn't have missed it for anything.'

'When did you get married?' Ashley enquired.

'Almost three years ago.' Giulia patted her stomach complacently. 'And this will be our third child.'

'Your third?' Ashley was quite stunned by the announcement.

Giulia laughed. 'I had twins the first time. You have a lot of catching up to do.'

Ashley managed a very forced smile, thinking how easy it was for some women to reproduce and how horrendously difficult for others. Bursting with health and vitality, Giulia actually made the process look simple, she thought painfully.

'Giulia's crazy about kids,' Vito delivered with a grim look, a betraying tautness etching his hard bone-structure.

Something snapped inside Ashley. 'Oh, shut up and go to hell!' she flared in a ferocious hiss, and walked off, fiercely keeping her anguish to herself. She was damned if she would ever tell him again. He deserved to be left in ignorance but she did not deserve the snide remarks.

'Ashley!' A man she was brushing past closed a hand over her arm and looked at her with surprise and pleasure. 'What on earth are you doing here?'

She blinked bemusedly as she recognised Josh's familiar, friendly face, and suddenly grinned. 'I could ask you the same question.'

'Oh, I've been on the guest list ever since I delivered Giulia's twins.' His bright blue eyes twinkled. 'She came over to London on a shopping trip and went into labour in Harrods, of all places. Instead of giving birth in the very exclusive clinic in Rome which she had selected, she ended up in a National Health hospital. So what's your excuse? Care to share it while we dance?'

She allowed Josh to fold her into his arms. Vito was so tall that she could see him across the crush. Even at a distance she could feel the dark force of his appraisal. Dear heaven, here she was actually fraternising at close quarters with a member of the forbidden species ... a *man*! She wondered whether she would be shot at dawn and whether she would be allowed a last request.

'I was a late arrival. Have you seen her yet?'

'Seen who?' she asked.

'Vito di Cavalieri's wife-to-be.'

'You're dancing with her,' she sighed.

'You're kidding me!' Josh held her back from him. Slowly he shook his head and his mobile mouth compressed. 'You're not kidding. How the blazes did you meet him?'

'A long time ago.' She saw his pain and impulsively leant up and pressed a kiss to the corner of his tight mouth. 'I'm sorry it wasn't you, but he's like a migraine that won't go away,' she whispered, belatedly realising that she had drunk just a little too much champagne since her arrival. 'Why can we never love the people we want to love, Josh? Why do we always have to love the wrong ones?'

'Nature made it that way to keep us all on our toes.' Josh skimmed a wayward strand of Titian hair from one perfect cheekbone and withdrew his hand not quite steadily. 'You're so beautiful, I can't think straight around you——'

'Then permit me to do your thinking for you, Mr Hennessy.' At the sound of Vito's smooth dark drawl, Ashley's head whipped round so sharply that it hurt. 'Put your hands on her just one more time and I'll break every bone in your body!'

As she spun, Vito clamped a hand that bruised round her forearm, his darkly handsome features a mask of rigidly constrained anger. She clashed with glittering golden eyes and paled.

CHAPTER SIX

'How could you do that to me?' Ashley gasped. 'How could you embarrass Josh like that?'

Wrathfully unrepentant, Vito poured himself a whisky from the decanter on the library table. 'I warned you. If I hadn't felt sorry for the poor bastard, I'd have hit him! *Dio*, what sort of a woman are you?'

'What's a kiss on the cheek?' she demanded. 'Josh is an old friend.'

'And presumably the bedsheets have yet to cool,' Vito breathed with stinging derision.

'I won't even dignify that with an answer.'

His sensual mouth was set in a cold line of austerity. 'He's in love with you. As a former victim, I'm an expert on the symptoms. Did you give him the same run-around that you gave me? Was he weak enough to beg? He's a fool. If anyone begs in our relationship, it will be you.'

She shivered, the bite of that menacing assurance making her skin prickle with fear. 'You'd have to kill me first.'

'No, *cara*,' Vito contradicted silkily. 'All I have to do is take you to bed. Something I plan to do over and over again in the very near future. It would seem it was a mistake to neglect you all week.'

'I—I don't know what you're talking about,' she muttered tightly.

'You looked across at me and then you were all over Hennessy like a second skin.'

A heady flush washed her complexion. Yes, she had known he was watching her, indeed had been aware with every fibre of her being. She was too honest with herself to deny the fact. He had hurt her and she had reacted as impulsively as she usually did. She was suddenly

93

ashamed of encouraging Josh to put himself in such an awkward position.

'So why did you do it?' Vito drawled.

Whipped on the raw once too often, she flung back her glorious head of hair and lifted her chin. 'Go to hell,' she said fierily.

'If I go to hell, I take you with me.' His strong, dark features taut with anger, he reached for her. 'I want to know why you found that cheap little exhibition necessary.'

A powerful hand was welded to her narrow shoulder, denying her the retreat she had been about to make. Involuntarily she collided with narrow dark eyes fringed by dense black lashes and the effect was paralysing. Her breath tripped in her throat. 'We should get back to the party...'

Vito ran a blunt brown forefinger up the extended line of her throat and she swallowed jerkily. The atmosphere was heavy, intense. Her mouth ran dry, her soft lips parting as she snatched in air. Heat was beginning to surge up inside her. Long fingers glanced caressingly along her jawbone and she had to fight the temptation to turn her cheek into his palm like a sensuous cat begging to be stroked. The hand on her shoulder slid down her rigid spinal cord, tracking her raw tension and then sinking into the narrow indentation just below her waist to ease her closer still.

'The party,' she repeated shakily, struggling to hold on to thoughts already blurred round the edges.

His brilliant gaze glittered over her wide eyes and tremulous mouth as his fingers spread over the curve of her hip and pressed her into the hard cradle of his lean thighs. Excitement, wild and inescapable, shock-waved through her. The bold thrust of his erection against her stomach electrified her. She quivered in response and shut her eyes tightly in soundless despair, wanting to feel revulsion, wanting to feel anything but this insane compulsion to uncurl her taut fingers and force him even closer.

'Why?' he persisted.

'Why what?' she mumbled, despising herself.

'Hennessy?'

'Giulia... you hurt me.' The words came in an unsteady rush.

His hands dropped from her and he stepped back, relocating his glass. He left her marooned in the centre of the carpet. Dazedly, she looked at him, the shock of separation shrilling through her nerve-endings with a butcher's efficiency. In the soft pool of the lamplight, he had the beauty of a dark angel but the hard, ruthless angles and sleek lines of a predatory animal. Neither, she registered dully, could have been more coldly merciless in administering punishment. And she was painfully reminded of how easily he had walked away from her once before.

Her legs were wobbling. Her stomach felt seasick but worst of all was that clawing hunger of arousal still clamouring for assuagement. She sank down on to a sofa, pale and drained and deeply ashamed that he could exercise such effortless power over her.

'You really do hate me, don't you?' The question that sought no answer simply slid from her tongue. 'And you blame me for everything that happened four years ago. You don't want to accept that the view is very different from my side of the fence.'

'Is it?' There was no emotion whatsoever in the flat response.

'You walked out, not me,' she condemned in an undertone. 'I needed to find somewhere else to live and I was broke——'

'The rent on that apartment was paid up until the end of the year,' Vito incised drily. 'There was no need for you to move out. I also opened an account for you so that you would not be short of money.'

'Yes...' A choky little laugh escaped her. 'I'll never forget that most sentimental of final farewells. A chequebook delivered by special messenger. Just what every woman wants as a last touching memory of your undying devotion. What did you think I was? Some little bimbo you had to pay off?'

An almost imperceptible flush demarcated his high cheekbones. 'I was responsible for you. I discharged that responsibility in the only way open to me at that time.'

'I didn't take your money when I lived with you. Why would I take it when you were gone?' she whispered hoarsely. 'I couldn't go back to the flat I'd shared because I sublet it two weeks before you left. That's why I ended up on Steve's couch...'

'The baby...was it mine?' He shot the question at her without warning. He was out of context but she could see by his stillness, his cold concentration that it was really the only topic he was ready to focus on. 'The subject is closed', he had said a week ago, but even Vito was human.

The raw cruelty of that question pierced her like a knife. And the strength of her own pain surprised her for she had believed that she was prepared for that suspicion. 'How can you ask me that?' she gasped.

In the smouldering pulse of the silence, Vito elevated a satiric ebony brow.

Ashley bowed her head, quivering with a hatred that was but a thin patina over a painful surge of confused emotions. Where was her anger? She wanted her anger, she needed that anger. But instead she was suffering a desperate sense of loss and futility. Why did it hurt so much to hate him? Why did she feel so terrifyingly vulnerable? Why all of a sudden did it matter so much that he believed her?

'It was yours.' She surrendered, despising herself for the weakness. 'And——'

'That's all I want to know,' Vito interrupted fiercely.

'But how did you know?' she demanded finally.

'I put a private investigator on you. I was curious.' Vito cast her a freezingly shuttered glance but one brown hand clenched into a fist in betrayal as he spoke. 'I believed that there was another man involved. In the end that angle was immaterial. Purely by accident, I discovered that you had a far more powerful reason for wanting me out of your life . . .'

Ashley flinched. He thought that she would have gone to any lengths to ensure that she had the freedom to dispose of their unborn child. It was a sordid picture and one she did not have the means to dispel. In her absence she had been convicted and sentenced four years ago and he was allowing her no right of appeal.

'You won't listen to me,' she pointed out strickenly. 'But I didn't have the abortion. I changed my mind. I had a miscarriage a couple of months later.'

'We should return to the party.'

'Vito, you can't do this to me!' she cried.

He expelled his breath in a savage hiss. 'It's in the past. Let us bury it forever. I should never have told you that I knew——'

'But you did,' she interrupted emotionally. 'So you can't bury it again!'

'We have to.' He surveyed her ashen pallor and his dark features tightened. 'I accept that I was mistaken in assuming that the decision you made cost you no pain. Clearly it did if the subject still causes you such distress, but you have to accept that we are each the products of a very different upbringing and I am as much a victim of that conditioning from childhood as you. I cannot change what I feel, but I can learn to put those feelings behind me. It is something I should have done a long time ago.'

In a passion of pain and bitter frustration, Ashley rose to her feet. Strive as he could, his judgemental attitude of reproach and a complete inability to understand emanated from him in waves. Hot tears brightened her beautiful eyes to luminescence. 'Why don't you put those feelings behind you and try concentrating on what you *should* be feeling?'

'Meaning?' he prompted drily.

'Where the hell were you when I needed you?' Raw emotion shrilled from the embittered demand. 'Where were you, Vito? I was nineteen years old and there was nowhere I could turn! You got me pregnant. You walked out. You married another woman. And you say that you l-loved me? Well, the only response I have for you now is...where were you, and where was that love when I needed it?'

He was rigid with shock, all the natural vitality bleached from his golden skin. His classic bone-structure stood out in harsh relief, his dazed dark eyes twinned nakedly with hers as he was finally forced to take account of his own sins of omission.

Ashley drew in a deep shuddering breath. 'You don't live in the real word, Vito. You never have and you never will,' she condemned. 'You have a loving, supportive family and an obscene amount of money. You know about as much about how the rest of us live as a cartoon character! In the whole of your life you have never been in a position where you had no easy choice. So, you can afford to have ideals set in stone. You've never had to wonder where your next meal is coming from or how you're going to survive...and that's when ideals get compromised!'

A dark rise of blood had banished his pallor. He raised a not quite steady hand and brushed away the tears streaking her cheeks. In one of those lightning-fast switches of mood that disturbed her, she found herself within an ace of throwing herself into his arms. The compulsion was so strong that she might have given in to it had not Vito abruptly withdrawn his hand and straightened again, having belatedly mastered the shocked turmoil she had briefly seen in his strained gaze.

A soft knock on the door prefaced Elena's carefully slow entry. 'I do hope I'm not interrupting, but there is a party out here lacking the two principal guests.'

'Ashley will join us in a moment.' Deliberately placing himself so that Ashley's distraught profile was shielded, Vito guided the older woman out of the room.

In the buzzing silence he left behind, she fought harder than she had ever fought for self-possession and calm. Somewhere a clock struck midnight, and she trembled beneath the awareness that in less than thirty-six hours she would be Vito's wife.

'We should reach the villa in another hour.' Vito settled back in his seat, having enjoyed a long and apparently effortless conversation with their driver, Bandu, in Sinhalese. The house in the hill country had been in the Cavalieri family for four generations. He had dropped that fact casually as they boarded the plane in London, modestly neglecting to mention that he also spoke the language.

Even after a nerve-racking hour, Ashley was still on the edge of her seat at the sheer death-defying style of driving in Sri Lanka. Bandu wove in and out wildly at what seemed far too great a speed for safety, jumping on his horn with gusto and making absolutely no use of any other form of signal.

Behind them an ox was pulling a cart piled high with pineapples, unconcerned by the jam building up to its rear. In front was an incredibly dilapidated lorry. A lanky youth was sleeping precariously on top of the sacks, quite unaware that a sack near him had come open and was dropping coconuts at regular intervals beneath their wheels. An ancient old man, balancing a basket of fish on his head, jay-walked out in front of them at an unbelievably leisurely pace and actually stopped to adjust the load he carried. Ashley vented a stifled shriek, certain they would hit him, but Bandu simply swerved violently and continued on.

'Driving in Colombo requires nerves of steel,' Vito commented with wry amusement.

Still shaking with reaction, Ashley suppressed a yawn.

'You are still tired?' Vito looked politely astonished.

'A bit.' Yet she had slept throughout most of that endless flight. Perhaps that was why none of this seemed real. The wedding had taken place yesterday and they had spent the night on the plane. She couldn't understand why she was still so tired. Possibly it was the immense strain of striving to accept that she was now Vito's wife.

It didn't seem possible. Ashley di Cavalieri. The Press had been outside the church, dealing yet another shock to her system. She had expected a very quiet wedding. True, Vito had not said it would be, but she had assumed that, since this was not to be a normal marriage, he would prefer a register office and an absolute minimum of frills.

As a result, she had been quite unprepared for the delivery and last-minute fitting of an oyster silk wedding gown and equally unprepared for the bouquet, the two hundred guests, the private party afterwards and the exquisite wedding cake flown in specially from Rome. Actually, by that stage, Ashley had gone beyond shock. She had played a starring role in the sort of grand bridal soap opera that she had never dreamt she would experience. At the back of her mind screamed the awareness that today, thanks to the power of the media, her entire family would learn that she had married.

Her mother would be deeply hurt by her total ignorance of the proceedings. Her father would be furious that that same ignorance would be equally obvious to their neighbours. Susan would be offended. And Tim? Ashley's soft mouth took on an anxious curve. Her brother would probably be very suspicious of the extraordinary speed and secrecy with which the marriage had taken place.

The streets, crammed to capacity with children, cattle, bicycles and every other possible form of transport, were now behind them. The narrow winding road climbed through coconut and cashew plantations. Rice grew in paddies along the way and in every direction palm fronds were etched like lacy sentinels against the deep blue unclouded sky.

A trio of dark-skinned girls, wrapped in colourful sarongs, stood washing themselves at a standpipe by the side of the road. Bandu braked to avoid the staggering steps of a naked little toddler stamping in a puddle near the pipe. Ashley grinned. Children were the same the world over. The attraction of water play was universal.

'What a beautiful child.' She craned her neck to catch a last glimpse of the engaging toddler.

'The Sinhalese are a very attractive people.'

Something in his tone made her turn her head. A questioning glint lit his perceptive gaze. Suddenly conscious that she had accidentally jettisoned her role of indifference to children, Ashley avoided his eyes and stiffened.

A few miles further on, the car turned up a steep, gated drive through a grove of cassia trees. Ashley climbed out into the hot, still air and dazedly studied the building before her. Dropped into an English village, it would have looked perfectly at home there. It had all the solid charm of a Victorian country house with the addition of a wraparound veranda to permit greater enjoyment of the tropical climate.

'My great-grandfather bought the estate from a British planter. I turned the tea plantation over to a workers' co-operative,' Vito explained. 'But I retained a considerable amount of land to ensure the seclusion of the house.'

An astonishing number of smiling faces were gathering on the veranda to greet them. Scorn in her eyes, Ashley whispered, 'Surely even your dignity does not require this number of staff?'

Vito sent her a stinging look of reproof. 'Employment is far from plentiful here. While wealth may cushion me from what you choose to call "the real world",' he derided in an undertone, 'I follow a policy of providing work for as many people as possible.'

Scorched by the rejoinder and flushed, Ashley was propelled forward to meet the staff. It was a long-drawn-out process. Such chattering friendliness could not be swiftly concluded. All but the youngest spoke good English and it was clear from Vito's questions that he was well acquainted with each and every one of them.

Another yawn crept up on Ashley. Seeing her stifle it, Priya, the small, rounded housekeeper, smiled and swept her upstairs into a large bedroom, full of beautifully carved mahoghany furniture in the colonial style. But Ashley barely had the time to admire it because the first thing she saw was a large photograph of Carina set in prominent position beside the enormous bed.

Quick as a flash, Priya registered the source of her sudden tension. 'You want that I should remove?' she pressed anxiously. 'I did not like to without instruction.'

'Oh, please leave it there.' Alarmed at being so easily read, Ashley forced a casual smile, behind which she boiled with a confusion of angry sensations. Were there photographs of Carina everywhere? Was she expected to lie in Vito's arms tonight with the saintly first wife staring down at her from the sidelines? A sense of deep humiliation and rage intertwined inside her.

After Priya had finished showing her the adjoining bathroom and dressing-room with touching pride, Ashley said that she wanted to lie down for a while and refused the offer of refreshment. She threw herself on the bed. That photograph, she reflected fiercely. There could be no stronger reminder that this was not to be a normal marriage. She rather thought that Vito, who excelled on small sensitive details when he so desired, would have tactfully banished the photos had this been a different sort of alliance. And why did she kid herself that Carina was the one on the sidelines?

It was she, Ashley, who was on the outside. If Carina hadn't died, Vito would still be with her. They would have had children by now. Dear God, why did she persist in denying the obvious? Why shouldn't Vito have come to love his first wife? They had shared so much: family, friends, background and outlook. He held her memory in the highest possible esteem and spoke of her only rarely but then with repressed but strong emotion. In every way they had been very well matched. Why couldn't she face up to the fact that Vito had loved Carina?

Until now she had flatly refused to accept that Vito
might have married for more than the 'right reasons'
supplied by their similarities. Jealousy and resentment
had blinded her. Once he had called Carina a very dear
friend. Ashley had been the infatuation, Carina the
woman he turned to and finally stayed with. And suddenly she was agonisingly conscious that all Vito wanted
from her was a baby and a quick exit from his life. From
the outset he had made it abundantly clear that that was
the only use he had for her now.

A small sound roused her from an uneasy doze. She
sat up abruptly as a lamp went on. Her stomach heaved
in protest, her head swimming. Vito, dark and devastating in a white dinner-jacket, surveyed her from the
foot of the bed. A slight frown pleated his ebony brows,
a look of spurious concern in his searching gaze. 'Are
you ill?' he enquired.

Swallowing hard on her nausea, she stared back at
him with loathing. Obviously her system didn't take to
jet-lag too smoothly, and not eating much in recent days
probably hadn't helped.

'I'll call a doctor.' Vito straightened with decision.

With a look of smouldering resentment, heightened
by her sense of being absolutely trapped, Ashley
snapped, 'I don't need a doctor! I just don't want anything to do with you!'

He absorbed the colour flooding back into her face.
'Dinner in half an hour, then,' he drawled succinctly.

'I'm not getting up,' she muttered, and rubbed her
hot brow. 'I'm so warm.'

'You can hardly expect to be anything else with the
windows closed, the curtains drawn and the air-
conditioning switched off.' Vito responded flatly and
strode into the bathroom.

She heard the gush of running water. 'I didn't know
there was air-conditioning.'

From the doorway, he tossed her a blessedly cool cloth
and she wiped her face with it blissfully. Sliding upright,
she smoothed her creased clothing, wishing she had had

the sense to undress before she lay down. Vito was surprisingly silent.

'I'll be down soon.' She sighed.

'How long have you been on these?'

Glancing at him, she froze. In one brown hand, Vito displayed three little boxes. Her supply of the Pill. Ashley was so shattered by the sight that her mouth fell inelegantly open. She couldn't believe he had them. They had been right at the very foot of her suitcase inside her toilet bag. 'Where did you get them from?' she demanded shrilly.

'One of the maids must have unpacked for you while you slept,' Vito breathed. 'They were sitting beside the sink.'

'I don't know how they got there,' she said stupidly.

'Perhaps you would like me to ask the maid?'

Ashley paled, her fingernails biting into her clenched palms. The silence went on and on and on, brick piling steadily on brick, and Vito wielded that horrible silence with merciless efficiency.

'We have an agreement.' Vito slid the boxes into the pocket of his jacket. 'And you are a cheat.'

'B-because what you're demanding is . . . is——'

'What you agreed to,' Vito incised unyieldingly. 'And I don't intend to be defrauded by technology.'

Agreement . . . cheat . . . defraud. The terminology of the business world and the law courts. Didn't he realise that she was a living, breathing human being ruled by emotion? Or didn't that matter? For him, emotion clearly didn't enter the equation. The week before last in London when he had made love to her . . . that, at least, had been full of emotion. Anger, bitterness, revenge—at least he had been feeling something. But now they were down to the bare bones of the cruellest contract and Vito had just shut down her one escape hatch.

'It will only be for a year.' The assurance was delivered harshly as though the sight of her emotional disturbance was unwelcome. 'If you don't conceive in that year, I'll let you go.'

A year. She squashed back an hysterical laugh of disbelief. A year. You couldn't even say he was prepared
to waste that much time on her. A year. She wondered
wildly if he would ask for his money back at the end of
the trial period. She refused to think about what would
happen if he was successful.

She came downstairs in an ice-blue Versace gown that
glittered under the lights. While she was dressing, she
had vaguely wondered where all the noise was coming
from. But, as Priya led her outside, the singsong rise
and fall of many voices ceased. They were to dine by
candlelight on the veranda but not in splendid isolation,
she realised, dazedly taking in the flaming coconut
torches set up to light a large circular arena in front of
the house. Like a stage, the rear was screened by a laced
fence of palm leaves.

As Vito pushed in her chair, he murmured, 'This is a
complete surprise to me as well. The staff arranged the
entertainment in honour of our marriage.'

They were about to enjoy a performance of the Kolam
Natima, a folk drama worthy of the theatre, he explained. A narrator made his appearance, two drummers
and a piper backing his entrance. One by one the dancers
appeared in glorious costumes and enormous masks,
playing the parts of gods, demons and other mythical
beings in a celebration of Sinhalese folklore. Ashley was
entranced and, although Vito translated, he oc-
casionally fell silent for some reason.

When Priya approached with two tiny glasses of a
liqueur made from arrack, Sri Lanka's favourite alcoholic beverage, Ashley asked, 'But what is Kolam all
about? I'm confused.'

Priya gave her a wide smile and chose to intervene on
Vito's behalf. Indicating the two most spectacular
masked figures, she said, 'This is the King and that is
the Queen. She desires to have a baby, no?' Giggling,
she stepped back into the shadows.

Stupid, how stupid she was! Reddening to the roots
of her hair, she belatedly read the significance of the

dancers' erotically symbolic movements. A very traditional drama for a newly married couple, she conceded. She refused to look at Vito.

A brown forefinger skimmed her clenched hand where it rested on the table. 'This wasn't my idea,' he reminded her.

In rejection she snaked her hand back out of reach, keeping her attention glued to the dancers below although in truth she could no longer see them.

'You're making this a fight every step of the way.'

'What did you expect?' she muttered bitterly.

'This is not the place for an argument.'

When the performance was over, Ashley smiled until her jaw ached. Vito requested coffee in the drawing-room. The evening was becoming an endurance test.

'Is giving a little so impossible for you?' He slung the demand with savage impatience as soon as they were alone.

'Yes.' She bent her head. Give a little, end up giving the lot. Vito would accept nothing less than complete surrender to his will. It would be a battle to the death. She saw no other course. She was fighting for her own emotional survival.

'*Dio*! *Madre di Dio*!' The sudden eruption of anger took her by complete surprise, so calm and so cool had he been over the past days. 'What do you want from me? The past *is* past,' he stressed fiercely.

'You're my past and you're here!' she shrieked back at him, losing control with a speed that shook her. 'I can't get away from you!'

'I have tried so hard to be reasonable,' Vito raked back at her. 'You didn't even smile for the wedding photos!'

Ashley loosed a wild laugh, seething at him from the back of a carved settee. 'If you want a smiling bride, you certainly don't need me!' she condemned explosively. 'You've got them all over the place in all your houses. Carina... everywhere I look! Surprise, surprise, there's another one on that table!'

Taken aback, Vito followed her accusing finger to the source. He flashed her a glittering appraisal. 'I'll have them all put away. Or would a ceremonial burning be more appropriate?'

'Meaning?' she launched back at him furiously.

'You're jealous,' he murmured very quietly, as though the idea was a positive revelation to him.

Halted on the tremulous edge of another outburst, she gritted her teeth. 'Insulted by your insensitivity,' she contradicted. 'But then, with your track record, that's nothing new to me!'

Slamming out of the room, she raced up to her bedroom and locked herself in the bathroom. As she peeled off her clothes and stepped under the mercifully cooling flow of water from the shower, she wondered why, in Vito's company, her greatest enemy was nearly always herself. She lost control, she opened her mouth too wide and that was usually that. When she emerged from the bathroom she expected him to be in the bedroom but he wasn't.

That infuriated her. She wasn't finished with him yet. Dragging the towel from her head, she started to ease a comb through the tangled mass of her hair. So absorbed was she in the task that she didn't hear him enter; she suddenly saw him in the mirror. Reaching over her head, he took the comb from her suddenly nerveless hand and calmly began to employ it with a dexterity that took her back four years.

'Don't do that,' she said weakly.

'It was insensitive of me to say it out loud. I should have savoured it in silence,' he drawled mockingly.

'Why don't you do us both a big favour and leave me alone?'

'But you know the answer to that.' His reflection threw back the reckless, dangerous glitter of the smile on his sensual mouth.

Ashley sat there like a statue while he removed the last snarl from her hair. But as his hands cupped her shoulders to slowly draw her up from the dressing-table, she started to tremble.

'This...us.' He seemed to savour the words. 'It's inevitable.'

Under that dark spell, she had to struggle to find her voice. 'Doesn't have to be.'

The sash of her robe slid free and she stopped breathing. Already she could feel the anguish of her body's anticipation. He pulled her back against him, burying his mouth hungrily in the curve of her arched throat, his hands sliding up her ribcage to find the aching fullness of her taut breasts. She moaned as expert fingers toyed with the prominent buds of her nipples, an unbearable spasm of excitement seizing hold of her.

'Why should you be able to fight it when I can't?' Vito demanded roughly, a husky, masculine growl of arousal in his accented drawl as he tugged her round to take her mouth.

CHAPTER SEVEN

THAT taunt powered Ashley's revolt. With a super-human effort she denied herself the drugging heat of his mouth and broke free. Twisting away, hating herself, she rubbed at her reddened lips as though she needed to cleanse herself of his touch. 'But I *can* fight it,' she swore, as much for her own benefit as his.

'Why fight yourself?' Vito murmured softly. 'You want me. I believe that you want me more than you have ever wanted any other man. That's why you fight me. With me...you feel threatened.'

The calm confident assurance banished the colour from her cheeks. 'And what book of pop psychology did you dig that out of?' she managed shakily. 'Don't think I don't know why you want to think that. From your point of view it's a very flattering interpretation.'

'Is it?' Mercilessly he held her eyes with his own. 'In my life many women have wanted me, *cara*. To be desired is scarcely a novelty.'

Hatred flashed through her. It was the truth. He had it all. Power, wealth, charismatic attraction and the kind of banked-down smouldering sexuality that magnetised the female sex. It had never surprised her that she had fallen madly in love with Vito. But the force of those feelings had terrified her. Her fragile security had been based on a need for total control of her own life. Instinctively she had known that, given the smallest opportunity, Vito would dominate her, making her choices for her, carving her up and rearranging her into the image he wanted.

'So what picked me out from the common herd?' she prompted with deliberate scorn.

A broad shoulder edged up in a graceful shrug. 'Your beauty, your individuality... and the little things——'

'Such as?' Defensively she folded her arms.

A faint smile softened the hard line of his mouth. 'The way you challenge me. The way you deliberately take the opposing view to mine in every discussion whether you believe in it or not. And you make me curious. You're like a Chinese puzzle box...'

A box he intended to open. A mystery he intended to solve. He scared her. Yes, she did feel threatened. He was already stripping away those layers he had talked about, denying her any hiding place.

Tilting his dark head back, he studied her with brilliant dark eyes. 'Why, for example, do you always take cover behind a large piece of furniture when we're having an argument?'

'I don't,' she denied and only then realised that she was standing on the far side of the bed, about as far as she could get from him and still be in the same room.

'You do. Once it outraged me, but now I'm used to it. Physically you're afraid of me and four years ago I found that incredibly insulting,' he confided, slowly closing the distance between them again. 'How can you be afraid of me when I have never once hurt you? Which brings me to the obvious question... who did?'

Pale as snow and trembling, Ashley let her lashes drop to conceal the ravaged turmoil suddenly brimming in her eyes. She was incapable of movement as he folded her into his powerful arms, his extreme tension lost on her for she was far too absorbed in her own.

'Because if I ever get my hands on him,' Vito grated in a savage undertone, 'I'll kill him.'

She had not been an abused child. At least she didn't think so. Slaps, shakings, occasional bruises from too forceful hand grips. Her father was a powerfully built man and she had often told herself consolingly that he didn't know his own strength when he lost his temper. But it hadn't been the fleeting physical pain that caused her the most damage... no, it had been the awareness that she was the only one of her family ever to incite that reaction from him. He had never struck her mother, her sister or her brother, was indeed loud in his disgust of other men who used physical force to subdue those weaker than themselves.

No, what had bothered Ashley the most had been the 'why me?' sensation. Why only her and not her siblings? And somewhere along the line she had started to realise that in her father's eyes she was somehow different, presumably different enough not to inspire the love he had for Susan and Tim. For he did love them. He mightn't show it, and Tim might be his favourite, but he did love them in a way he had never loved his younger daughter. Banishing her from the family circle had cost him nothing . . . she was painfully aware of that fact.

'Who did it?' Vito demanded.

Her lashes fluttered and she came back to life again. 'You're imagining things,' she whispered.

'I thought I might be until I saw your face.' Long fingers cradled the tender curve of her jawbone. Golden eyes alight with fury were pinned with naked obduracy to her vulnerable features. 'Who?' he persisted.

Had she been an innocent, she reflected sadly, she might almost have believed that he really cared. Hot tears pricked her eyelids and she couldn't understand why his response should make her cry. 'It . . . it was a long time ago,' she muttered. 'Leave it. Some things are private.'

'Not between man and wife.'

'I'm not your wife!' she rebutted fiercely.

His hand tightened on her shoulder, imprisoning her. 'You are my wife, and the sooner you accept that fact, the happier you'll be. And while you're working on that,' he advised, 'accept at the same time that I will never use my superior strength to hurt you.'

A long shudder ran through her. There were worse kinds of pain he could inflict. The sort of pain that left no visible mark. Four years ago he had been remarkably adept at that brand of cruelty. How could she cope with a male so brilliant at penetrating her defences? How could she fight this ridiculous deluding sense that somehow it was a relief?

'Some day you're not going to need to fight me any more,' he told her levelly. 'Some day you will learn to trust me.'

'You're not just ambitious, you're a megalomaniac.'

'I just don't like failure,' he countered darkly. 'And somehow at some stage, without even realising that it had happened, I failed with you.'

The admission sent chill sparks of dread down her taut spine. What more did he want from her? Love? The undying devotion he had sought in the past and been denied? Helplessly she shivered, shrinking from an awareness of how complete would be his revenge if she fulfilled that aspiration. And she was vulnerable. Wasn't it time she faced that truth? He was holding her close and there wasn't a cell in her body failing to fire to that proximity. Below her breastbone, her heart was pounding like crazy.

'Failure,' he repeated huskily as he drew her unresisting figure down on to the bed. 'A black spot of dishonour on a perfect record. I can't live with it.'

With every word he reinforced her deepest fears.

Casually he lifted her slender hand. He pressed his lips mockingly to the platinum band on her wedding finger. 'Does it feel like a manacle?'

Breathing rapidly, she said, 'A stranglehold. A symbol of possession. I'm surprised you don't want Cavalieri tattooed all over me in case I stray!'

'You won't be straying, *cara*. I'm very careful with my possessions.'

'Damn you!' she began, trying to sit up.

He ran the tip of his tongue down the valley between her breasts in an erotic foray only halted by a meeting with the towelling edge of her robe. She fell back again, momentarily stunned by the rush of heat fired by that most calculating preliminary.

'*Dio*...I almost forgot.' Reaching behind him, he produced a familiar little box. One-handed, he deftly opened it and extracted a tiny pill. 'Medical science does have its advantages. I thought about them over dinner and I'm prepared to compromise——'

Bewildered, she parted her lips. He dropped it in and automatically she swallowed. 'But you——'

'We don't need it to happen this soon. Success might conclude other pleasures that are for the moment...for me at least,' he conceded raggedly, 'far more important.'

An odd little twinge of pain coloured her relief at his change of heart. He could not have told her more clearly that for him pregnancy would be a sexual turn-off, or possibly the final act of the whole charade he had involved her in.

'Aren't you pleased?' he probed.

'Ecstatic...but you want everything I've got to give in return,' she whispered tightly, understanding that, for this present forbearance on his part, there would be a price.

A questing hand closed over one small firm breast and her eyes slid shut in an involuntary reflex, every tiny muscle tautening beneath her skin in a hot rush of anticipation.

'And that's incredibly generous, isn't it?' he said thickly. 'Considering that I could take it without asking.'

His other hand skimmed down the pale length of her thigh and her senses leapt wildly. Her own hands dug like talons into the embroidered bedspread beneath her, so fierce was the temptation to touch him. She would submit, that was all. Nothing more, nothing less.

Laughing softly, he divided the robe, bent his dark head over her quivering stomach and let his mouth roam over her responsive flesh. 'I'm going to drive you out of your mind,' he promised.

Shedding the twin of her own robe, he rearranged her on the bed as if she were a doll. She collided with the rapacious hunger glittering in the all-male appraisal devouring her pale body, lingering on the swell of her breasts and the sleek curve of her hips. And she burned all over, self-conscious in one sense but strangely proud in another.

She was breathing very fast as she looked up at him, her tormented green gaze wandering from his broad shoulders down to the rough curling hair defining his muscular chest and beyond to his hard flat stomach. About there, she closed her eyes tightly, willing herself into stillness and silence.

He closed his mouth round a rosy nipple and teased her with his teeth. A whimper of stifled sound escaped her. She felt the erotic pull deep in the pit of her stomach like a key turning in a lock. He leant over her, delving his tongue between her soft lips and plundering the response she could not withhold. She was shaking, alternately hot and cold with the force of her own arousal. It had happened so fast, she couldn't control it.

His slim hands moved over her with ruthless precision, now hard, now gentle and always, always one agonising step behind where she needed them to be. She couldn't stay still, she couldn't stay quiet. He was slowly and inexorably working down her quivering length, leaving no part of her untouched. His teeth nipped playfully at a sensitive spot on her thigh and her back arched, the heat building to a cruel pitch as his fingers toyed with the damp auburn curls crowning her most tender flesh. She moaned out loud, choking back his name, panting for breath.

'Let go,' he demanded. 'Or I'll make you let go.'

And then he did what she had never allowed him to do before, something so intimate it was unbearable, something so exciting, it drove her right off the edge. Parting her locked thighs, he buried his mouth against that most secret place and tasted her, and after that there was nothing she could do but feel. A primitive avalanche of wild sensation took over and wave upon wave of explosive pleasure shuddered through her in an earth-shattering climax of passion that took all else before it.

'You're mine, absolutely, unequivocally mine.'

Not quite sure she was even conscious, she felt her eyes cling to him as he knelt at her feet, surveying her with triumph. Hard hands curved to her hips as he pulled her to him and there wasn't a resistant bone in her body. He drove into her hard and deep until she didn't know where she began and he ended. Her heartbeat slammed into overdrive as he set a savage rhythm. Her skin, slippery with sweat, slid exquisitely against his and she was suddenly, incredibly at fever pitch again, her finger-nails raking the smooth damp skin of his back in that instant of raw, electrifying pleasure that freed her from the chains of the mortal world.

Afterwards, it was a long time before he released her from his weight. And she didn't want him to move. She wanted him to stay where he was forever. She felt glorious, and at the back of her woozy mind she knew that sensation wasn't likely to last.

He rolled free and lay back for a few brief minutes, silent, in a damp golden sprawl of satiation on the other side of the bed. Incautiously she leant her chin on her elbow and looked at him, only to realise that his attitude of relaxation was highly deceptive. His superb bone-structure was starkly apparent beneath his dark skin, grim tension etched into the forbidding line of his mouth. Without warning, he leapt off the bed, snatched up his robe and shrugged into it.

She couldn't believe that he was just going to walk out after what they had just shared. Indeed, she let him get as far as the door before she was provoked into speech. 'I'm sorry, sir. Did I disappoint you?'

Lightning-fast, he spun back, the black brilliance of his gaze stabbing into her. 'That isn't amusing.'

Her eyes wide to hold back the scorching moisture welling up, Ashley retorted, 'It wasn't supposed to be. But I shouldn't have to tell a male of your experience that there's a certain form for these occasions——'

'And you would know all about that, wouldn't you?' His nostrils flared with distaste. 'How many other men have there been?'

She went white and regretted challenging him, but pride had demanded that she refuse to allow him to treat her in such a fashion. He had said that she was his wife. A husband didn't make love to his wife and then get up and leave her to sleep elsewhere without a word or even a gesture.

'Tell me,' he invited rawly. 'I want to know.'

'I don't think now would be the most auspicious time,' she said thickly, choking back the humiliated tears clogging up her throat.

'My imagination runs riot,' he intoned harshly. 'I'd prefer the truth.'

'You wouldn't recognise the truth if it bit you.' Tense as a bow string, her eyes huge in her drawn face, she whispered, 'I won't allow you to treat me like this. You said...you said the past was past——'

'How the hell can it be, when every time I touch you it comes alive again?' he slung back at her fiercely between gritted teeth. 'Do you think I want to feel like this? Do you think I enjoy lowering myself to ask such degrading and shameful questions?'

'What do you want? A list of names, places and times?'

Beneath her appraisal he went satisfyingly rigid.

'M-maybe you'd like me to score the names on this list,' she stammered, sick with revulsion.

All the angry colour was wiped from his taut features.

'Tell me, what was that you said about trusting you?' she muttered. 'Even four years ago, you didn't trust me.' She forced herself to look squarely back at him. 'And do you know why? I made this colossal mistake of being what you then called gloriously spontaneous and what I still call gloriously stupid. I went to bed with you the first night we met, and you're so buried in your medieval code of what constitutes a decent woman that you can't ever forgive me for that. It doesn't matter that you were my first lover. The whole time we were together you were just waiting for me to do it again with someone else. And don't think I didn't know that!'

As she fired that final sentence unsteadily at him, she slid off the bed at speed and took refuge in the bathroom, shooting the bolt home on the door.

'Ashley... come out of there.'

Wordlessly she shook her head, tears running down her cheeks. This time he had gone too far. She had allowed him to go too far. But at no price was she prepared to live however briefly with a hypocritical, judgemental swine, who made her feel unclean. 'Do you think I'm proud that I can't keep my hands off you?' he had demanded in London. No, she could quite see, as he swiftly removed himself from her contaminating presence after satisfying his own lust, that he wouldn't be proud.

'Ashley...'

She switched on the shower purely to drown him out. A long time later she crept out, no precise plan in mind except a fierce, overwhelming need to get away. Hurriedly she dressed, selecting a starkly cut white shift dress and a cerise jacket. After digging a few essential items into a beach-bag, she tiptoed out of the room and downstairs. The house was in darkness. The front doors were not even locked.

As she came down the steps from the veranda, a white-clad figure rose from the shadows. 'Lady go out? Lady want car?'

It was the middle of the night but his gap-toothed smile seemed to say that the eccentric habits of Europeans abroad were not worth even a show of surprise.

'Yes, car,' she agreed, delighted it was going to be so easy. 'I want to go to Colombo.'

'I get Bandu. Take time.' He looked anxious now.

'Can you take me?' Ashley asked hurriedly, envisaging the whole household being aroused.

'Me? Kumar?' Slapping his chest, he named himself and laughed with positive delight. 'Yes, I take lady. Kumar very good driver,' he asserted.

The fact was not immediately apparent in the way the car lurched round the side of the house but Ashley didn't waste any time in climbing in. Slamming his foot down on the accelerator, he thundered down the highway and they shrieked out on to the road on two precarious wheels.

'Could you drive more slowly?' Ashley gasped.

'Very slow, Kumar go very slow.'

They raced down the road at what felt like ninety miles an hour. Kumar was curved round the wheel like a racing driver.

'Slow!' she finally shouted in terror about ten minutes later when she recalled the drop down to the tea terraces on the outer edge of the road. Kumar jumped on to the brakes in an emergency stop. The car skated out of control from one side to the other. The nearside wheel hit the ditch and the car careened into a skid before finally lurching to a halt. Ashley was screaming. Kumar was screaming even louder. The car rocked. Silence fell.

'Go slow, have accident,' Kumar groaned. 'Not go slow in movies, go fast.'

Undoing her seatbelt, Ashley staggered out on to the road and threw up in the ditch. She was shaking all over in reaction and was only dimly aware of her companion's shouted monologue of woe in his own language until a tremendous grinding noise drew her attention. In the moonlight, she stared in disbelief as the car simply rolled off the edge and went crashing down on to the terraces below. Kumar had forgotten to put the handbrake on. The steep incline had done the rest.

He gave a great shriek of horror and threw himself down on the road. He was in such a state that it was some time before she could reassure him that he would not lose his job and that Vito would not blame him for the loss of the car. He was unconvinced, his misery making her feel guiltier than ever.

Finally she managed to establish that there was a small rest-house some miles down the road. They started to walk. It took an hour and the heel snapped off one of her sandals when she went over in a pothole. By the time Kumar had roused the owner of the rest-house and the portly owner, soon joined by curious wife and excited children had heard the whole story, it was three in the morning and Ashley was wondering how on earth she could have been so crazily impulsive.

She was shown with warm hospitality into a small, sparsely furnished room. After washing at the cold tap over the ancient corner sink, she slid between the patched but scrupulously clean sheets and stared up into the white blur of her mosquito net.

Wasn't she a clever girl, then? But then, when had she ever been clever with Vito? Inexorably her thoughts turned back the years and found no comfort in the past either...

The morning after that fateful party she had persisted with her assertion that she never wanted to see Vito again right up until it came to the point of actually leaving him. Then grudgingly she had allowed him to drive her home. He had asked her out to dinner that evening. She had told him she was busy. He had suggested the following evening and she had told him that she would be busy for the rest of her life.

And he had laughed and said nothing. But that night he had simply arrived complete with an enormous bunch of roses. Her flatmates had been struck dumb. She had reasoned that it wouldn't be cricket to shoot him down in front of an audience, so she had gone to dinner.

'You really don't have to do this,' she had kept on saying, as prickly as a cactus in his company and ordering scrambled egg on toast in the five-star restaurant because she didn't want him to spend his money on her.

'Every day I start with a clean sheet,' she had told him. 'Last night? It never happened. You don't owe me anything.'

'Why are you so determined to drive me away?' he had finally asked.

Clearly it was a very new experience for him with a woman. He had switched on the charm with a smoothness an oil slick would have envied. Last night...it had happened too fast. He was older, wiser, should have known better. It was all his fault, his responsibility, and he wanted them to start over as if it hadn't happened.

'Why?' she had queried baldly.

A wry smile had formed on his beautiful mouth. 'I think I've fallen in love with you.'

'Lust,' she had countered stiffly. 'Fallen in lust.'

'I also think that I'm going to marry you if you ever keep quiet long enough for me to ask you,' he had drawled with complete confidence.

That had shaken her, but she had quickly decided that he could not possibly be serious. Even so, she had spent the remainder of the evening explaining in no uncertain terms why she would never marry him or anyone else.

'So we have an affair,' Vito had murmured with immovable calm.

'I don't have time for an affair.' She had been seriously rattled.

An ebony brow had quirked. 'You will find time for me,' he had responded without a single doubt in the world.

And he had been right. But between them they hadn't found quite enough time, she conceded with wry hindsight. No two people could have had less free time available. Banking, at the highest level, was a very demanding career. With barely an hour's warning, Vito could be off to Europe for an unspecified number of days. Ashley had had her classes, her course-work to complete and the necessary hours she put in as a waitress to keep the wolf from the door. And she had also had male and female friends she didn't intend to drop entirely for his benefit.

Although the plan had been that they would start over and get to know each other properly, it hadn't worked out that way. The frustration of their conflicting schedules had meant they scarcely saw each other the first three weeks, and when he took her back to his apartment one lunchtime passion had, quite without prompting, once more flamed out of control. They had never actually discussed living together. He had suggested that she use the apartment when he was abroad to study in peace away from her crowded flat. Piece by piece her possessions had drifted over there, and night after night Vito had contrived to ensure that she didn't go home.

But no sooner had she begun hanging her clothes in one of his wardrobes than the disagreements they had frequently had had escalated into full-scale rows. Now that Vito really knew her schedule, he expected her to drop the commitments that he considered either unnecessary or unimportant. The fact that she insisted on holding on to her waitressing job had outraged him. He had never understood that she could only cope with the vast disparity between their finances by ensuring that she did not live off him like some parasite.

Her equal determination to retain her friends and attend occasional student functions had infuriated him as well. At the outset he had been irritated, but when one evening he chose to join her and discovered her sitting at a table with a male friend, irritation had become outright jealous, possessive suspicion.

When Vito had a relationship with a woman, he expected twenty-four hour exclusive rights. If he wasn't available, he had expected her to sit at home weaving little-woman dreams about him and hanging by the phone waiting for his call.

The rows had become increasingly more passionate and destructive. A case of the irresistible force and the immovable object. Neither of them had been prepared to give an inch and Ashley had become more and more insecure, dismayed by how harrowing she found it when Vito was angry with her, trapped by the awful truth that she just didn't have the strength to walk away from him. More and more the bedroom had become the only place where they were ever in complete harmony.

When he criticised her, argued with her or even attempted to reason with her, she had started to slam out of the apartment. She'd begun to lie awake nights worrying while he slept like a log. One of her tutors had told her plainly that her work was no longer up to

standard. Her concentration was gone. All she'd thought
about was Vito...Vito...Vito. He had tried to help her
with her work but when one evening she had blamed
him for the problems she was having he had lost his
temper and told her that she was out of her element in
accountancy because she couldn't seem to grasp the in-
tricacies involved.

He had apologised, but she had known that he was
telling her the truth, and bitterly had she resented hearing
it from someone as effortlessly brilliant in the financial
world as he was. It had driven another wedge between
them, and then, when they were at daggers drawn, he
had disappeared off to Italy one day and taken an entire
week to actually phone her.

Elena had visited the day before he returned. And Vito
had returned with an ultimatum. He was moving back
to Italy. His father was ill. He had family and business
obligations that could not be dealt with from London.

'We'll have to get married,' he had said over his
shoulder, breaking off to instruct his housekeeper to pack
for him.

'It's time you grew up,' he had said.

'I want a family while I'm still young enough to enjoy
them,' he had said.

'I am really bored with this feminist sh...rubbish,'
he had said.

'You have to accept that my position in the bank and
my responsibilities quite naturally take precedence over
yours,' he had said.

And when it had finally penetrated—and it had taken
a long time—that she was not biting off his hand in her
eagerness to grab that generously offered golden ring,
he had said, absolutely incredulously, 'But you've been
sharing my bed for months!'

A blazing fight had ensued. Ashley had told him a
few home truths, the sort of home truths he had never
heard before. For someone who loved to dish out
criticism, he had been amazingly over-sensitive. In a
nutshell, he had gone through the roof. Everything she

had ever done to annoy him had been dug up. Everything she had ever failed to do to please him had been resurrected. Even in her anger, she had seen that Vito truly believed that her entire world should revolve round him.

The iron hand had emerged from the velvet glove with a vengeance. For five months Vito had really been babying her along, humouring her, controlling that cuttingly cruel tongue of his, presumably with the greatest of difficulty. For when that glove had come off she discovered that he could demolish her every argument in scathing one-line sentences and make her feel really, really stupid and weak. She had seen her mother, head bowed in submissive silence, and she had seen herself reduced by Vito to a similar level . . . and that vision had petrified her.

Shifting on the hard mattress, Ashley slid back to the painful present. She got up after eight. Vito would know that she was gone by now. Dully she wondered where she had imagined she could run. Not only did she have a duty to ensure that Kumar didn't suffer for her foolish flight in the middle of the night, she also had the lowering awareness that, even had she made it to Colombo, she would have been leaving Sri Lanka with a great bleeding wound where her heart had once been.

Her heart didn't just beat a little faster when Vito was around. It jumped up and down and did acrobatics. As her host showed her to a rickety table overlooking the tumbling waterfall at the rear of the property, she was again blinking back the tears she so despised.

Around dawn it had hit her, the truth she had fought so hard to deny. A huge blinding flash of unwelcome enlightenment. There had been so much pain since he came back into her life that she had floundered in bewilderment and a near constant emotional overload. She loved Vito. Only love could give him the power to hurt her this much. Had she ever really hated him? Right now, she didn't know. She was too devastated to think of anything beyond the fact that loving him, the way he felt about her now, was a death sentence.

A faint sound made her head fly up from the menu she was studying. She froze. Vito was standing on the bleached boards of the sagging veranda. He was unnaturally still, his pallor pronounced. One brown hand was fiercely clenched in the cream jacket he had discarded. A white shirt was carelessly open at his throat, his thick black hair damp and tousled, and a most uncharacteristic black shadow of stubble marked his tense jawline.

Slowly he swallowed, incredibly intent dark eyes clinging to her startled face. 'I thought you were dead,' he breathed roughly.

CHAPTER EIGHT

VITO tossed back a large glass of arrack brought by their bustling host before he spoke again. The fiery liquid seemed to revive him. The harsh lines of strain engraved between his nose and mouth smoothed out. The natural colour gradually returned to reanimate his dark, taut features.

'Priya woke me up to tell me that a car carrying a European woman had gone off the road last night. Then she informed me that you were gone——'

Ashley paled. 'I'm sorry.'

'When I saw the car, I knew nobody could have come out of that alive.' He continued to stare at her as if he still couldn't quite accept the evidence of his own eyes. 'I came in here to find out if they knew where...where you had been taken——' His uneven tone cut off harshly.

'Kumar and I got out before the car went off the road. He forgot to put the handbrake on.' An uneasy laugh bubbled in her throat but she didn't let it escape. 'The accident wasn't his fault.'

'Like hell it wasn't!' Vito ground out. 'He has no driving licence. He could have killed you!'

'He can't drive?' Ashley was shattered and then she thought back to the previous night's conversation. Kumar had offered to get Bandu and she had asked him to take her instead. He had been both flattered and excited by the request. 'That didn't occur to me. I was very pushy,' she added hurriedly. 'I insisted that he take me. You can't blame him. He was only trying to please me.'

Vito contrived to look both unconvinced and uninterested at one and the same time. 'I'll leave him to Priya. He's her nephew. And she's a holy terror when she's roused.'

'He won't lose his job?' she persisted.

'You're alive. I'm in a forgiving mood.'

She took a deep breath. 'Are you? When my brother was at fault, you were ready to send him to prison.'

'Kumar doesn't have a sister I wish to marry,' Vito quipped humourlessly. 'I shall choose to forgive instead.'

'You're probably wondering what I'm doing here——'

He signalled their hovering host. 'I was depending on you to make our wedding night a little out of the ordinary,' he incised in a smooth aside. 'Let's have breakfast. You haven't lived until you've sampled hoppers.'

The cup-shaped pancakes made from a batter of rice flour, palm toddy and coconut milk came with a variety of delicious fillings. Ashley was surprised to realise that she was really hungry. They finished up with guava and passion fruit and beautifully fragrant tea.

Vito's silence troubled her. After all that had happened, the last thing she had expected him to do was sit down and eat a good meal. Awkwardly she cleared her throat. 'I expect you think I'm really a cheat now. We had an agreement——'

'But I haven't been fulfilling my part of it,' he cut in flatly.

'It's been an emotional time for us both,' she muttered unhappily.

'But I haven't been making it any easier. I had no right to pry into your past last night and no excuse to taunt you.' He surveyed her with grave, measured emphasis but a betraying tautness edged his sensual mouth, revealing that he didn't find it easy to make that admission. 'After all, I'm no celibate myself.'

'It was understandable.' Suddenly, now that he was giving ground, she found herself pathetically willing to forgive. She gritted her teeth on the discovery, reminding herself of the need to be cautious. The last thing she needed right now was for Vito to guess how she felt about him. The only thing she had left was her pride.

'I've had a mistress for the past eighteen months.'

The announcement paralysed her. She bit her tongue and tasted blood.

Vito released his breath audibly. 'I finished it a few months ago, but do you know what attracted me to her?'

Nausea stirred in her stomach. Vito was not of the confessing variety. She really didn't know why he was doing this and she desperately wanted him to shut up, because she did not want to be forced to think of him making love to another woman.

'She had hair the same shade as yours,' he proffered in a raw offering of deep self-contempt. 'But she wasn't you.'

'No. She wouldn't have gone charging off down a mountainside in the middle of the night and crashed your car, I guess,' she muttered tightly.

'Nobody but you would do that,' he pointed out in an almost gentle tone, and in a gesture that was curiously clumsy for one of his grace he narrowly missed toppling a cup as he reached for her hand.

The heat of his fingers engulfed her smaller ones and she bent her head. She wanted to tell him that she had never had another lover. She focused instead on the tumbling gush of the waterfall, shining with blinding brilliance in the bright sunlight. Not only did he not require that information from her, he would also very probably refuse to believe her, and every time he refused to believe it hurt just that little bit more deeply.

'I'm five days late with this but I still need to say it,' he breathed. 'The night of the party you hit me hard with what you called the view from your side of the fence——'

'I don't want to talk about that.' It was her turn to interrupt and deny him the opportunity to have her listen. The baby... that subject was too painful in the light of his disbelief.

'Ashley...'

'No!' she said fiercely, sharply withdrawing her hand from his.

'We have to talk about it.'

'But I don't want to!' Snatching in oxygen, she rose unsteadily upright, ready to run if he persisted.

'Maybe it's too soon,' he conceded with surprising generosity.

Perhaps not so surprising, she allowed when she thought about it. He had been badly shaken by the sight of that crashed car and the conviction that, if she had not been killed she was at the very least severely injured. But for how long would this greater gentleness and understanding last?

Ten days later, she stood on the heights of the ramparts of the Dambulla Cave Temples, her bare toes heated by the sunwarmed ground, and conceded that Vito was making a very real effort to be well-mannered, entertaining and non-controversial. She was beginning to learn that in some ways she had not known Vito at all four years ago. That annoyed her but it was true. For a start the charm wasn't switched on, it was entirely natural. The tension that had once underscored their every moment was gone now that all sources of possible confrontation were banned.

He was far more conservative than she had ever appreciated. The way he had swept her off her feet the night they met had distorted her image of him, much as it had distorted his image of her. She could see now that in the past she might well have put Vito and his traditional values through one hell of an emotional wringer. She had gone out to well and truly shock him every time he roused her temper—a pattern learned in defiance of her father. But that pattern had been highly destructive. If Vito had been guilty of a desire to dominate and control, she had been equally guilty of replying with provocation. It had only inflamed the situation.

She stared out at the panoramic view of the citadel of Sigiriya, the giant monolith of red stone that rose hundreds of feet into the sky from a flat plane of scrub jungle. Lord, she was hot, despite the straw sunhat Vito had insisted she wore. She rubbed at the perspiration beading her face and suddenly realised that she felt pretty sick and giddy. It had been an incredible climb up to the temple and then their guide had spent so long giving them a tour of the astonishing wall and roof paintings.

'Do you think I could get a drink of water?' she whispered.

Vito stopped midstream in his conversation with the tiny wizened Buddhist priest in his saffron robes, reminding her of yet another unknown facet of his character that had lately been revealed. He was not the crashing snob she had once assumed, nor was he a workaholic with nothing on his mind but his next big deal—although four years ago he had seemed very much that way.

'You look terrible,' he murmured, pinning a supportive arm to her bowing spine.

'The heat...'

He took her over to the shadows by the wall. 'I shouldn't have brought you up here.'

'I'll be OK in a minute.' She was embarrassed by her own physical frailty. Until she had come to Sri Lanka she had truly believed that she had the constitution of an ox. But this wasn't the first time she had felt that she had overdone it. The day before yesterday and the day before that she had had a similar episode of wobbly knees and nausea, although on both those occasions she had contrived to conceal her weakness from Vito.

He was taking charge, fussing over her. Having sat her down on a step, he reappeared with a paper fan and proceeded to wield it most efficiently. He looked in his element, she thought wryly: big, masterful, rudely healthy male reviving poor weak little woman. He liked to be needed, and she had never allowed herself to need him before. She thought of Elena with her deliberately fluffy manner in his radius, his sister, Giulia, guilelessly fluttery, and decided that experience hadn't prepared him very well for a woman of independence.

They made the descent in easy stages. He took her into the shabby little café in the village and bought cold drinks. 'We'll sit here for a while before we get back in the car,' he decided.

'Sightseeing is more demanding than work,' she sighed ruefully.

Vito tensed. 'I suppose you miss your career.'

The pretences she had put up now seemed so futile in retrospect. 'It wasn't exactly a career.'

'You never talk about it,' he remarked with studious casualness.

'There's not a lot to talk about.' She sipped at her drink.

Dark colour overlaid his aristocratic cheekbones. 'And naturally you blame me for that. I know how much your career must mean to you. If...I mean——' unusually, he faltered '—when we part, I'll give you whatever assistance you require to re-establish yourself in an appropriate position. I have many contacts.'

'Take it from me, Cavalieri influence would be overkill.' She spoke through stiff lips. When we part... Last time a cheque-book, this time a new job. Whatever you want, I can give you, he might as well have said...but he couldn't give her what she most wanted. She felt sick with longing, sick with self-disgust. He hadn't touched her since that night. He said goodnight to her after dinner every evening and went off to his computer terminal in the study he used as an office while she went to bed alone. He stayed up to all hours, seeming to thrive on just a few hours' sleep. Was the idea that she had had other lovers really that distasteful to him? Or was there a far less complimentary reason behind his unexpected restraint? It was perfectly possible that he no longer found her desirable. Familiarity bred contempt, didn't it?

'Where exactly were you employed?'

'Nowhere you would know.'

'Why are you being so secretive?'

'Look!' She took a deep breath and murmured wryly, 'I dropped out of university, Vito.'

He surveyed her in disbelief. 'You what?'

'I failed my exams.'

'Failed?' he ejaculated with flattering astonishment.

Baldly she issued the facts.

'But why didn't you resit your exams?'

'I wasn't well and my father withdrew his support.'

'Why?'

'Because he found out that I had been living with you.'

Succinctly he swore. 'Isn't there a student loan system available?'

'I was already in a lot of debt, Vito. With no support from home there was no way I could manage to survive and study at the same time.'

He was very pale. 'And still you wouldn't take my money. The view from your side of the fence grows more distressing with every word you say.'

She had upset him. Yet revenge should have made him gloat. He had deeply resented her ambition once, not because he was uncomfortable with ambitious women but because she had apparently put ambition higher on the scale than him. 'It's all water under the bridge now.'

'So how have you lived?' he demanded grimly.

'Like everyone else, I work. For a while, I worked in a store. Don't be such a snob, Vito!' she snapped, seeing him flinch.

'I am not a snob,' he ground out. 'But I am understandably very disturbed by what you have told me.'

'Oh, come off it. If you'd still been around when I'd failed, you'd have loved it!' Ashley condemned bitterly. 'It would have saved you the trouble of telling me that my needs and ambitions came a poor second to yours. But I wasn't surprised, Vito. When I was seventeen, my father told me when I wanted to learn to drive that if God had meant women to drive they would have been born with wheels! The two of you would have been good company for each other in the prehistoric caves!'

'I have no intention of trying to defend myself when you are in this mood.'

'I think a defence would really tax your ingenuity.'

She refused to speak to him all the way back to the house. It was childish, but she relished the chance to get her teeth into some resentment and use it to hold him at bay. She might be in love with Vito, but that didn't mean she had forgotten what a ruthlessly selfish swine he could be. There had never been a worse mismatch of personalities, she told herself.

'We're too alike,' he sighed.

She blenched, wondering whether he could read minds into the bargain.

'Both hot-tempered, strong-willed and self-centred.'

'I am not self-centred.'

He slanted her an incredulous look. 'In the entirety of our relationship four years ago you never gave a single thought to how I might feel about anything. You told me how you felt. You told me what you wanted. You told me what you would do. Never once did you consider how I might feel.'

She was shaken by his censure, unwillingly recalling how defensive she had been, how aggressively determined not to compromise in any quarter.

'And because I loved you I played the game, but playing the game by someone else's rules never came naturally to me,' he delivered. 'If I don't win any awards for retrospective sensitivity, it was not entirely my fault.'

'You never loved me.' She picked fiercely on the one bit she could argue with, refusing to concede defeat.

He didn't bother to combat the accusation and she wanted him to, which in turn angered her more. Of course he hadn't loved her. A man in love didn't immediately run off to marry another woman. But in the midst of that thought came a stark acknowledgement of other facts, facts she should have put together sooner. Vito had believed she was living with Steve. Wouldn't that have been enough to convince him that his future would never lie with her? And that Carina, familiar to him from childhood, would make a far more suitable wife?

Not that that excused him for abandoning her as completely as he had. How could he have so easily accepted that she had turned immediately to another man for comfort? Then he had indicated to Ashley that he had had considerable doubts about her even before he had grounds for such suspicion. Possibly it had been a relief to find an excuse to exclude her completely from his life. But that exclusion had made him bitter.

The second week of their stay drifted lazily past. Ashley had taken to lounging by the swimming-pool in the afternoons, napping under the shelter of a huge umbrella. Vito was spending more and more time in the study. She was starting to feel like the untouchable woman and the tension was building again, resulting in stilted sentences and lingering silences. The lack of sex was probably getting to him, she reflected painfully. Even if he wasn't tempted in her direction, Vito was a very virile man and the frustration of their situation had to be annoying him. It really was the most peculiar honeymoon.

Bored, she walked into the house in search of another magazine. Priya was struggling to arrange flowers in the hall with a complaining toddler clinging to her knees like a limpet.

Grinning, Ashley bent down. 'Who's this?'

'My youngest grandchild, Nuwan.' Priya sighed wearily. 'My son-in-law, he is in hospital in Kandy and my daughter has gone to be with him.'

'Nothing serious, I hope?' Ashley was busy making interesting shapes with her hands to attract the little boy's attention.

'An appendix. The operation is today.'

'Let me take him out into the garden. It's such a beautiful day.'

Priya protested, but the enthusiasm with which the child was greeting Ashley's advances was not lost on her. Nor had it escaped her attention that her employer's wife was eager for something to do.

Two hours later the only sound in the lush grounds was Nuwan's tinkling laughter as Ashley played with him. Half an hour beyond that, he had fallen asleep with the suddenness of the very young, curled up in her arms, trusting that he would be held in comfort until he chose to wake. Priya brought out a tall glass of lime juice on a silver tray and clucked at the signs of weariness on Ashley's face.

'You should rest, madam,' she fussed anxiously. 'It is not good for the baby for you to be too tired.'

As the sleeping child was retrieved by his grandmother, Ashley froze. Priya wasn't referring to her grandson.

The little woman gave her a teasing smile. 'You think I don't know?' She laughed. 'I have eleven children and twenty grandchildren. I am very wise to the coming of new babies...he wonder why you tired all day, he wonder why you don't want this food...that food. And it is in your face. How do you say? A fullness? I see it. I know. You tell him soon, make him very happy man.'

As Priya trudged back to the house, Ashley drew in a deep, shaken gasp of the hot still air. It wasn't possible. But it was possible, a little voice crowed. That night in London when that desperate yearning passion had overwhelmed every other restraint. Shock made her break out in nervous perspiration. She hadn't thought, she hadn't dreamt, she hadn't even wanted to consider the risk she had taken that night.

And now all of a sudden it seemed obvious. She had been so taken up with the complexities and strains of their relationship that she had been blind to the evidence of what was directly beneath her nose. The nausea, the dizziness, the exhaustion. None of them as pronounced as they had been the last time, but then this time she had been able to rest and relax, waited on hand and foot as she was. Some frantic calculations were required before she could gauge the likelihood of conception. Dazedly she appreciated that her period was ten days overdue.

'I watched you with Priya's grandson.'

Her head spun, pink washing her cheeks. Lean and darkly tanned in denim cut-offs that moulded his narrow hips and long, muscular thighs, Vito looked quite staggeringly attractive. With difficulty she dragged her eyes from his rawly masculine physique. 'I thought you were working.'

'I didn't marry you to spend my days locked into a computer.'

No, he had married her to have a child and then for some unfathomable reason had temporarily shelved that ambition. A ludicrous urge to laugh threatened her shaky composure. She was still deep in shock over the awareness that she might already be pregnant. His change of heart had come too late to save her.

But, even as she thought that, an ache of maternal hunger stirred in her, an ache as old as time. She stifled it, forbidding herself any images of warm, cuddly little bodies. Even if she was pregnant, she was convinced that she would very probably have another miscarriage. Bitter pain assailed her. How could he put her through this again? The agonising disappointment and the sense of failure would be all the keener a second time.

In the unresponsive silence, Vito murmured in measured tones, 'For a woman who doesn't like children, you're remarkably talented at entertaining them.'

The remark was explosively unwelcome. 'I never once in my life told you that I didn't like children!' she slammed back shakily. 'And why shouldn't I be good with them? That's the job I trained for... or it was my job until you came along and wrecked that as well!'

Vito's bewilderment was palpable. 'Your job?'

'I was working in a children's nursery.' Stuffing her feet into sandals, she set off down the sloping lawns towards the trees.

'And why couldn't you tell me that before?'

Brown fingers had captured her slim forearm to hold her still.

Furiously she thrust his hand away. 'It was none of your business!'

As she left the dark cloaking cover of the trees, he caught up with her again. They stood in a verdant sunlit glade where a natural pool had formed, fed by a mountain stream. It was a hidden place, a peaceful haven where the lush vegetation was allowed to riot and the orchids to bloom, safe from the taming lawnmowers and clippers that kept nature in order in the more formal gardens. Somewhere she could hear the raucous screech of a peacock calling to his mate and in the background still the fluttering wings of all the exotic birds they had disturbed in their noisy passage.

She clashed with the smouldering darkness of his brilliant eyes. 'Can't you understand that I want to be alone?'

'Greta Garbo you're not. Stop moving away,' he bit out warningly.

Angrily she halted that instinctive retreat, although she felt intimidated by the sheer size of him this close.

'I can see that giving you space was a mistake.'

'And what's that supposed to mean?' she demanded nervously.

His nostrils flared. 'I left you alone in the hope that you would use that time to come to terms with our marriage but all you have done is withdraw from me again. I wanted you to acknowledge the bond between us and come to me...'

'Bond?' she echoed. 'Come to you?' She went off into gales of wild laughter at the very suggestion that she might have approached him. Would he have expected her to walk on coals of fire afterwards as an encore? It seemed that nothing short of craven, crawling surrender would satisfy Vito.

A flash of naked fire lit his gaze as he stared down at her intensely vivid face. 'Don't,' he said softly.

'Don't what? Don't laugh?' She felt vaguely unhinged, as though he had somehow set her adrift.

The pure male vibrancy of his dark, set features merely increased her need to fight him. 'Do you really think I don't know how you feel? You want to scratch and claw me like a tiger to keep me at a distance but it won't work,' he spelt out. 'This marriage isn't a contest. It's not about winners or losers. In fact, were you to win on the terms you believe you want now, I wonder just how long it would take you to appreciate that, after all, you had lost...'

Involuntarily she was finding herself trapped by the golden blaze of his eyes. 'If you knew how I felt, you wouldn't be talking about losing. I hate you!' she swore vehemently, still sufficiently in control to defy him.

'No, you're afraid to trust me,' he contradicted arrogantly. 'You don't hate me.'

'I hate you!' she repeated wildly. 'I hate you! I hate you!'

Ashley was trembling. She could see what he was trying to do to her now. At the outset she had asked herself which was stronger, his desire for a son or his desire for revenge, and on their wedding night he had answered that question for her by postponing the first so that he could concentrate on the latter. Something akin to terror was snaking through her: the horrific thought that Vito would dismantle her defences brick by brick until finally he had her so completely in his power that he would know that a great deal more than physical attraction held her to him.

'I'll never love you again! Do you hear me?' she launched at him stridently, recklessly.

Disorientatingly, a brilliant smile softened the fierce line of his mouth. 'I should corner you at least twice a day and make you lose your head. By the end of a week, I'd know you inside-out...every secret...every thought. So, you believed that you loved me in your way, if not in mine, four years ago?'

Aghast at what she had conceded in temper, she began to swing away from him.

'You're not going anywhere.' A powerful hand intercepted her before she could move.

In the grip of absolute desperation, she lifted her arm and aimed a hefty slap at him. Vito tipped his head back and unbalanced her with remarkable agility, strong hands clamping round her waist to push her back on to the grass. Finding herself unexpectedly in a supine and far more vulnerable position, Ashley made a violent attempt to dislodge him. Vito laughed uproariously and pinned her flat, trapping her flailing hands in both of his. 'Uh—uh—uh!' he scolded. 'You are in a panic, aren't you? Hit and run. The last resort in your repertoire.'

Like those of a tiger cub at bay, her green eyes were on fire with defiance. 'Why are you doing this to me?'

Momentarily a wry look of acceptance seemed to cloud his unashamed amusement. 'I can't seem to get close without getting physical. So be it, *cara*. All your space just took a hike. I've withdrawn a privilege which didn't seem to be gaining me any ground.'

Her heart hammering crazily against her ribs, she gazed up into the implacable dark features suspended mere inches from her, suddenly starkly conscious of the scanty nature of her bikini. Still holding her hands flat with his, he took her mouth with all the savage hunger of a male who felt he had been exercising an unnatural and unappreciated brand of restraint.

A stab of raw sensation fired in the pit of her stomach. His tongue penetrated deeply between her lips, fanning the fire into a positive blaze. He went on kissing her until her lips were bruised and red and her bones were melted honey beneath her burning skin. Only then did he pull away and brush aside the bikini bra with impatient fingers, immediately bending his dark head to rub his mouth erotically across a taut pink nipple.

'I want you unbearably,' he confided. 'I want you so much that when I take you it will be like dying and being reborn.'

She moaned, her head thrown back as his hands cupped her breasts in a fierce possession. He rolled over and, catching her clenched fingers, drew them down to his taut, flat stomach, pressing them against the button on his waistband. 'I want everything the way it was,' he admitted raggedly. 'I want to wake up at dawn with you making love to me.'

'No,' she whispered breathlessly, vivid sexual imagery from memories she had buried deep living again inside her mind. But her body was already betraying her. The need to touch him as intimately as he touched her was a torment of desire fighting the last remnants of her control. Theirs had never been a one-sided loving. Dimly it occurred to her that in bed they had been true partners, neither one of them giving or taking more than the other.

He claimed her parted lips in a glancingly sweet caress that was a torment to senses already roused to a frightening pitch of excitement. In an unashamed admission of need, he pushed her hand against the hard bulge of his manhood, constrained by the unyielding denim, and the hunger that surged up inside her was uncontrolled. 'This...this I will have,' he breathed unsteadily, 'though you deny me all else.'

He was trembling, the sheen of sweat on his smooth golden skin testifying to the extremity of his arousal, and she knew then with a wild flash of satisfaction that he was no more in control than she was. But that wasn't what made her move closer and send her lips whispering over the flat male nipple she discovered amid the black, silky whorls of hair clouding his broad chest. That wasn't what made her skate teasing fingers across his unbelievably taut abdomen and feel him jerk and groan beneath her caresses. No, what drove her was the all-encompassing knowledge that in this he was hers, absolutely and completely hers in a way that he would never be any other woman's, and that was in that moment as powerful and seductive as the strength of her own desire.

With every inhibition released, she became a creature of alluring abandon, glorying in her own freedom. When the seducer became the seduced, the lines that had once divided them blurred until there was nothing between them but a mutually exclusive passion that burned out of control throughout what remained of the daylight hours.

It was as though they had never been apart, but even in the past their loving had never been so passionate or intense. When he finally settled between her thighs, she reached up to cup his damp cheekbones and claimed a tempestuous kiss as her right; those lines had faded altogether. As lost as she in the grip of that voracious desire, he shuddered and groaned deep in his throat in response and then he entered her wildly, deeply, and proceeded to make love to her with a thoroughness that exceeded her most colourful fantasies.

When it was over, she lay with her head against his chest, listening to his heartbeat still racing against her, gloriously at ease and at peace in the imprisoning circle of his arms. It was like dying and being reborn, she thought weakly, and afterwards it was like waking up in paradise, so intense was the release from her own body. For the first time she felt really close to him, so close that the first fingerings of alarm entered paradise and she tensed.

Vito tightened his hold on her instantly, smoothing a caressing and confident hand over her small head as if he were soothing a restive child. His touch felt tender, gentle, and was extraordinarily comforting. She remembered that, in all her life, the only time she had ever felt safe was in his arms.

'Maybe at the end of the year I might consider tempting your kid brother with another Ferrari.'

The illusion of paradise shattered into shards that pierced her flesh in all the most tender places. Like a madwoman, she found herself wanting to weep and shriek and tear at her hair in a painful ecstasy of despair.

She couldn't go back. She couldn't go forward either. The past would always intervene. Vito had the forgiving qualities of a Cesare Borgia. And he would stand by the last letter of that unholy agreement.

CHAPTER NINE

'IF YOU were a feline, you'd purr like a motor, *mia cara*.' Planting a teasing kiss to her brow, Vito straightened from the bed. Fully dressed and emanating waves of disgusting energy, he smiled down at her. 'I suppose you won't consider stirring yourself and having breakfast with me for a change?'

'No.' Her answer was muffled by the sheet and she was holding herself still as a statue, too well aware that the moment she attempted to sit up would also be the moment when she was most likely to throw up.

He chuckled and strolled across the room with all the lean, lazy grace of a hunting animal, replete after a good meal. 'I'll see you later.'

The last time she hadn't been this sick. The doctor at the hospital had said that her lack of sickness might well have been a sign that her pregnancy was unstable. The assurance had been small comfort four years ago, and at that rate this dreadful nausea she was presently suffering ought to be an indication of the most stable pregnancy of all time!

Priya appeared with a dry biscuit and a cup of aromatic herb tea. It was very hard to eat lying flat but Ashley did her best. The older woman muttered worriedly about her needing to see a doctor and Ashley ignored the advice. This morning scene had become routine ever since Priya found her being violently ill in the bathroom, and with a little bit of quick thinking Ashley had turned her into a partner in collusion to conceal her condition from everyone else in the household. She had lost a baby before, she had forced herself to confide. This time she didn't want to raise Vito's hopes unnecessarily, she had said. Priya had

142

understood such a motive. In her culture men were to be protected at all times from upsetting experiences. That was a woman's duty.

Oh, yes, no doubt at all, she was pregnant. She required neither test nor examination to confirm the fact. Already her breasts were swelling and incredibly sensitive, and if she hadn't been convinced that it was far too soon for her waist to start expanding she would have sworn her skirts were getting uncomfortably tight. Maybe she would blow up like a balloon by the third month, she reflected miserably. For how long could she hope to keep her secret?

Vito shared her bed every night. Vito made love to her every night. For that matter, Vito made love to her in the afternoons as well. In fact, this was just about the only time of day when he kept his hands off her. And she liked it that way, in fact she loved his constant hunger for her, revelled in this one hold she had over him, basic though it was.

Overflowing with self-pity, she blinked back tears and sniffed. She ought to be ashamed of herself. She should have told him a month ago that she might be pregnant, and then in all likelihood he would have left her alone. If she had any pride at all she would have long since grabbed at the first excuse she had to keep him at a distance. The trouble was...well, the trouble was that she might be living in a fool's paradise but she was so happy. She had never been this happy before, and she managed that feat entirely by blocking out the fact that this was not a normal marriage. She took each day as it came.

But tomorrow they were returning to London. The honeymoon would be over and all she had to look forward to was a miscarriage and the certainty that once that happened Vito would see the writing on the wall and let her go. Unless she could manage to hide that from him as well. Maybe it would happen when he was abroad...or maybe it wouldn't happen at all. She rested her palm protectively against her stomach. She wanted the baby so much that it hurt and no way could she have both Vito and the baby. She would have to go away and have it somewhere where not even all the Cavalieri wealth and influence could contrive to find her. Somewhere like the moon or Mars, she thought crazily.

Just before lunch she came downstairs, breathtakingly beautiful in an emerald dress as green as her eyes, an inner glow blazing from her lovely face so powerfully that Vito faltered in the conversation he was having on the phone. He caught her hand, planted a kiss in the centre of her palm and returned his attention with visible difficulty to the phone.

'It must be the air here,' he murmured, dark eyes almost dazedly pinned to her radiance. 'You get more gorgeous with every passing day.'

'You're just susceptible.' She looked like a cat contemplating a large, rich bowl of cream as she studied him, possessiveness surging through her veins in a heady surge. She couldn't take her eyes off him, either. There was a powerful electrical charge in the atmosphere. It lit her up like a high voltage shot of energy.

'*Madre di Dio*, you're going to kill me,' he whispered, mesmerised by her sensual smile.

She bit into a luscious grape, headily conscious of the effect she was having on him. So, on his side it was only the best sex he'd ever had . . . so what? She loved him. She was willing to settle for second best, willing to live for today at the expense of bitter regret tomorrow. If this was the only happiness she was fated to have in her life, she was ready to grab it with two greedy hands.

'I want my lunch,' she said.

'And it's our last day,' he reminded her with obvious reluctance. 'You said you would like to see the elephants again.'

The elephant orphanage at Pinawella had entranced her the previous week. He had remembered. The perfect companion and lover, entertaining, thoughtful and intelligent enough to be a constant challenge. Yet this same male had abandoned her, thought the very worst of her, married another woman, whom he still never mentioned though Ashley had given him several encouraging openings to do so. Sometimes, like now, these two opposing views of Vito's character tortured her, and yet she was afraid to get too close to the past lest it divide them again.

'I could always look at the photos I took instead.'

'And perhaps we could stay out of bed long enough to talk,' Vito tacked on tautly. 'I have things I need to say to you.'

He looked serious, and these days the minute he got serious she got nervous. Her appetite for lunch all but vanished. She pushed her food round the plate.

'Why is talking so threatening to you?'

'We fight.'

'We don't need to fight,' he drawled levelly.

'You make me feel like a child waiting outside the headmaster's study.'

'I don't want to make you feel like that, but we do have to learn to practise greater honesty with each other.'

'Why bother?' she demanded brittily. 'I'll be gone in another few months...won't I?'

He tensed. Dense ebony lashes briefly fanned down to meet his hard cheekbones. 'Yes, of course, but surely that does not negate the point of establishing better communication now?'

Equally tense, she snapped shakily, 'You're never satisfied, are you? You want to scour the fine print for a flaw to dwell on. I try to give you what you want and it's still not enough! I know it's only an illusion, what we have right now, but——'

'Is it?' Grim dark eyes rested on her.

She reddened. 'Of course it is.' Proudly she thrust up her chin, fearful that he was already suspicious of her motives and determined to conserve her own pride. 'I'm just giving you good value for your money!' she told him.

He went white beneath his dark tan. Desperately she wanted to reclaim the lie but it was too late. He rose from the table with a searing look of distaste that she was certain would live with her to her dying day. 'When I need a whore, I'll go to one, but you certainly deserve a bonus for your enthusiasm!' With a derisive hand he tossed a tiny soft leather bag on the table in front of her. 'For services rendered above and beyond the call of duty.'

He vaulted into the four-wheel-drive in front of the house and raked down the driveway out of sight. Trembling, she opened the bag. A flawless cornflower-blue sapphire set into a ring tumbled out on to her palm. The stone was quite exquisite; she knew that it was a gem of the highest quality, worth thousands and thousands of pounds, and the knowledge made her feel worse. It was a personal gift, unlike the engagement and wedding-rings demanded merely for the sake of appearances. She burst into floods of tears.

It was after nine when he returned. She was waiting for him in the drawing-room. When he appeared in the doorway, she shot to her feet. 'I didn't mean it. I'm sorry!' She hadn't intended to sound quite that pleading, but one glance at his dark, unsmiling profile was sufficient to panic her. What they had, she cherished. She could not face losing it.

'Forget it,' he advised chillingly. 'You get what you pay for. And since I did pay for you, I can hardly object to your candour.'

'Where have you been all day?'

'You actually sound like a real wife.'

Vito, I love you, please don't do this to me. She almost said those words out loud. She wasn't prepared for it to end yet. She wasn't ready. Maybe she would never be ready, she registered fearfully, if the second he walked out of the door in a temper she turned to a jelly. That was the extent of his power in the cruellest and most refined form, and she was in torment.

He poured himself a drink, offered her one, and when she uttered a negative said flatly, 'Why don't you go to bed? We're leaving early in the morning.'

'I didn't mean what I said.'

'Relax, your little brother was off the hook weeks ago.'

'That isn't why I'm trying to reason with you.'

'No? Well, there's only one other option, isn't there? The threat of a night without a sexual orgy thrown in appals you? Tell me,' he demanded raggedly, belatedly making her suspect that he was not enjoying his first drink of the evening, 'from the depths of your endless experience of my sex, am I really so good that you're prepared to crawl and beg?'

Every scrap of colour fled her face, leaving her bone-white. 'I . . . I don't really know. I've never had anyone else,' she whispered strickenly, shattered by his cruelty.

'The odds aren't in your favour, *cara*. Four years ago, I saw you in that bastard's arms in the street. Saw with my own eyes,' he stressed savagely. 'If I'd got out of my car, I'd have murdered you!'

'F-four years ago?' she stammered. 'You saw me with Steve . . . in the street?'

'Do you need to see it in writing?' he derided.

'B-but that means you must have——'

'Come back after you said no to the proposal?' he incised with icy bite. 'I did. I was a real sucker for punishment in those days. No more.'

She was trembling all over. 'But you couldn't have seen anything happen between Steve and me!'

'You were in his arms and you were bedding down in his flat.'

And abruptly it came to her when he must have seen her. The day she had discovered she was pregnant. She had started to cry in the students' union bar and Steve had flushed her out at speed. On the way back to his flat, she had told him what was wrong and he had put his arms around her. 'For goodness' sake, all he did was hug me . . . try to comfort me because I was so upset about the baby and you!'

'In that order, I notice. The horror of the baby, then me.'

Something snapped inside Ashley. That crack was the last straw in the state she was in. She stalked across the room and clutched him by the lapels of his Armani jacket. All of a sudden, she was a raging fever of emotion.

'That was the day I found out that I was pregnant and I was climbing the wall!' she lashed out. 'And you dare to tell me that you were sitting somewhere close by in a car, letting him do what you should have been there to do? Instead you were spying on me, dreaming up filthy suspicions on non-existent evidence? How dare you tell me that now? How dare you? You should be too ashamed to admit that you came that close and wimped out last minute!'

Her vehemence clearly astounded him. 'I didn't wimp out!' he raked back between gritted teeth.

'Oh, didn't you?' Although he was a foot taller, Ashley glowered wrathfully up at him as though she was the one with all the physical advantages and not he. She had such a fierce hold on his jacket that he would have had to break her fingers to shake her off. 'You wimped out, all right. You didn't love me enough, Vito. You didn't trust me enough. You put your rotten stinking pride first!'

'That's a——'

'And then, to crown it all, you went and married another woman when you still belonged to me! Do you think that I am ever going to forget or forgive that? You owe me, Vito... you owe me for every morning you wake up without a knife stuck between your ribs!'

Still in a tempest of unrestrained emotion, she jerked her hands away from him. Her frustration and her pain were so great that she literally didn't trust herself not actually to strike him now that she finally knew what had kept him from her four years ago. A silly, trivial misinterpretation of events, an almost laughable mis-understanding that had none the less blown her life and her hope of happiness right out of the water. But Vito had still been cool-headed enough to carry out a damage limitation exercise on his own life—that was what hurt her so much. In her imagination she could think of a lot of things that Vito might reasonably have done or felt then, but not one of them covered barely catching his breath and turning round immediately to ask another woman to marry him!

'I didn't love her.' The confession was reluctant, low-pitched as if only the silence dredged it from him.

And at last her bitterness was vindicated but most ironically it didn't make her feel any better. He had loved her but he had still married Carina. He just hadn't loved her enough, and that knowledge couldn't even begin to cauterise her wounds. Another revivifying surge of fury came to her rescue. She had suffered so much for so little.

'Want to talk some more, Vito? Want to continue establishing better communication?' she demanded tremulously. 'You didn't love her but you married her——'

'You didn't want me,' he reminded her harshly.

'Oh, you fool!' Ashley gave a stark laugh of rampant disbelief. 'Don't you know when a woman loves you? I said no to marriage and six children before I was twenty-five...I did *not* say no to you!'

Vito looked dazed. That aspect of that final hostile confrontation had evidently never occurred to him. '*Dio*,' he said thickly.

The artificial stimulus of rage suddenly ebbed, the tears threatening. 'I'm going to bed,' she told him shakily.

'Ashley.' As he spoke, she reluctantly turned her head back from the door. His grim smile was edged by the darkness and the shadows of the too recent past. 'Does it ever occur to you that we were both guilty of making remarkably hasty and stupid decisions?'

'You had more choices than I had.'

'I asked you to marry me because that was the only choice I had,' he countered levelly. 'I could not stay in London and I could not take you back to Italy as anything other than my wife.'

She shot him a scornful look. 'You didn't *ask* me to marry you, you told me that we would have to get married.'

'I told it as it was.'

'Your whole attitude . . . it was an ultimatum, a list of what you wanted and what I was expected to accept.'

He emitted a laugh, devoid of humour. 'Was that how you saw it? I knew that you didn't want marriage but it was all I had to offer. Hearts and flowers would have made the proposal even more ludicrous in your eyes. Nor was I in the mood—our entire relationship had followed lines outside my experience. I had just learnt that my father had only months to live——'

'You said he was ill . . . you didn't tell me he was dying!' she condemned.

'You didn't seem very interested either way.'

Guiltily, she flushed, recalling her hurt, defensive state of mind the day after his mother's visit. Where his family was concerned, she had not been in a charitable mood.

'I was already angry and bitter,' Vito confessed tautly. 'My father had asked me to marry Carina—in spite of the fact that I had already told him about you! It was very much in the line of a last request from a dying man. We had an extremely violent disagreement on the subject. It was the only thing he could have asked of me that I could not do——'

'I didn't know.' She was shocked, realising that in wishing to marry her Vito had withstood far more than mere family opposition. His elderly father had made a most unreasonable demand and Vito had stood his ground and refused, but the distressing background to that refusal must have cost him dear. Vito came from a close and loving family. Conservative as he was, he had probably until that moment been a most loyal and dutiful son, who had never caused them an ounce of concern. Now she understood the strongest motive behind Elena di Cavalieri's interference. Her husband had been dying. She had fully believed that Ashley could not make her son happy. Those two hard facts had driven her into an attempt to break them up.

'What difference would it have made to you? You say that you loved me,' Vito drawled with derision, 'but you must have known how impossible it would have been for us to try and conduct a long-distance relationship——'

'Maybe I would have liked the option!' Ashley snapped back.

Vito elevated a satiric dark brow. 'Maybe I might have given you that option had you not made it so insultingly obvious that you did not see our affair in a permanent light. Always you were saying to me... if I were to meet someone else... if you were to meet someone else!'

Ashley lifted her chin, temper igniting afresh. 'I thought I was too young to make any promises. I didn't want to feel tied down——'

'So you made me feel like a regular one-night stand instead!' he slated savagely.

'I thought that was my line!'

'You were scared a better prospect might be waiting round the next corner.' Vito cast her an outrageously offensive smile. 'Seemingly, there wasn't.'

'A man came low down on my list of priorities, and when I listen to you now I know exactly why!' she scorned furiously. 'I offered you an open, adult relationship and you couldn't handle it!'

'And how well would you have handled it if I'd walked in the door one night and casually dropped that I'd met someone else?'

Her expressive face dropped a mile at the prospect.

'You didn't know the first thing about being an adult,' Vito slanted back at her with cutting emphasis. 'You wanted me, but you didn't want the commitment that came with me. All you ever gave me was sex, bloody stupid arguments and hassle!'

'Th-thank you very much!' Her voice throbbed, her eyes wide to stem the scorching tears behind her lids. 'I know where to come for a reference, don't I?'

'And the only reason I'm getting more this time around is that——'

'—you're a lousy domineering bully, who never ever thinks about my feelings!' she spat, and hared out of the room, taking the stairs two at a time.

Vito strolled out into the hall and angled his dark head back. 'By the way, there won't be any locks on the bathroom doors in our house in London. What are you going to do?' he mocked. 'Do you think you might actually find yourself in the frightful position of having to share those feelings with me?'

A slammed door was his answer. Ashley flung herself on the bed. The fire of her emotions was exhausting her now. She glanced up, ready to unleash another barrage, when a soft knock preceded the opening of the door. When Priya appeared, she scolded herself for imagining that Vito might knock on his own bedroom door.

'I hope I will not offend,' Priya began anxiously, the door still ajar behind her. 'But you might have fallen on the stairs and hurt the baby——'

Ashley groaned. 'You're right . . . but just for a minute I forgot about the baby——'

'It is not wise for a woman to forget when she is carrying a child,' Priya persisted. 'Calm and care at all times are most advisable. When I saw you, I was so afraid you would fall.'

'I won't do it again.' Ashley was annoyed with herself for having let temper take over again. But even as she thought that, she stiffened and tensed in dismay as Vito filled the doorway. Priya bowed out at speed.

'What do you want?' she demanded, wondering in horror if he could have overheard them discussing her pregnancy, but there was no shade of any sudden comprehension in his dark features although his appraisal was intense.

'To say goodnight?' he queried teasingly.

'Goodnight!'

*   *   *

'Interesting as your mother's gynaecological history no doubt is, Mrs di Cavalieri——' Mr Beckett began.

'Brown!' Ashley reminded him again, feeling foolish when he raised his eyes heavenward in silent suffering. 'I require complete confidentiality. I don't want anyone to know that I'm pregnant,' she added shakily, emerging from the room where she had been dressing.

Mr Beckett abandoned names altogether. 'As I was saying, your mother's misfortunes have far too great a hold on your imagination. Frankly, I'm more concerned about your state of mind than your health. Your pregnancy checks out exactly as it should for the first trimester and as I've already told you taking the Pill for a couple of weeks won't have done the slightest harm to your baby. But you're a tiny bit underweight. Hopefully that problem will take care of itself as the sickness recedes. Would you like to sit down?'

Stiff-backed and tense, she took a seat. 'What's wrong?'

He sighed heavily. 'Nothing is wrong. If you'd looked at the scan as I suggested——'

'I don't want to get too attached to the baby.'

'If you intend to be my patient, I absolutely refuse to listen to any more pessimistic remarks,' he delivered. 'As for not wanting anyone to know that you're pregnant— I'm afraid that will be rather difficult in a shorter time than you expect. You see, you are expecting not one baby but two—— Nurse!'

Ashley had almost fallen off the chair, faint with shock, and had to endure having her head pushed down between her knees. Twins—she couldn't believe it! Twins! As she started to tabulate all the extra risks involved in carrying twins, she felt even more giddy.

Josh was waiting outside on the street for her. She tottered down the steps, as pale and drawn as an accident victim. 'What are you doing here?'

'Is that any way to greet an old friend?' He pressed her into the taxi he had waiting. 'You were so secretive on the phone when you asked me to recommend someone, I was concerned.'

'I'm pregnant!' she gasped.

'Congratulations, luv!' the cab driver said.

'Twins,' she hissed tragically at Josh. 'And there's none in my family!'

'They run in Vito's.'

'They won't run with me for long.'

'You really are upset,' he finally registered.

He took her to a fashionable restaurant and she poured out her heart, a handkerchief in one hand, a glass of unadulterated spring water in the other.

'Why aren't you sharing these terrors with Vito?'

It was a reasonable question. But how could she be honest with a man who was planning to take her baby away from her? On all sides she felt constrained by secrecy, and the awareness that she would not be able to conceal her condition for much longer tortured her. She would have to leave Vito far sooner than she had planned. 'I can't tell you.'

'Is he treating you badly?' Josh breathed furiously, and clasped her hand.

She gulped bravely behind her handkerchief. Actually he was treating her very well, but not like a wife, more like a maiden aunt. Any sex appeal she had ever had had clearly vanished virtually overnight in Sri Lanka. They had been back in London for ten days and she had her own bedroom all to herself. He had flown to Milan five days ago and he hadn't even suggested that she might go with him. Sex, bloody stupid arguments and hassle, . . . evidently his intelligence had prevailed over his animal instincts, for the best he could seem to offer her now was amazingly polite conversation and horrifically considerate behaviour. Yes, on her terms, he was treating her very badly.

'No, he's very kind.' Her mouth wobbled again. 'He's killing me with kindness. We haven't had one argument, not even a teeny weeny disagreement. He agrees with everything I say. All the passion has died.'

'Some men find pregnancy a little hard to adjust to——'

'My, my, my, what have we here?'

Josh removed his hand from Ashley's with complete cool and glanced up at the smirking youth standing by their table. 'Hello, Pietro,' he said drily.

'Tell me, Auntie, do I mention this to my uncle or do we keep it our little secret?' Pietro sneered.

'Go away, you little creep,' Ashley snapped in a raw undertone. 'Or I'll knock your teeth down your throat!'

Taken by surprise, Pietro's cool front was cracked. With burning cheeks, he threw her a look of hatred and said, 'You haven't heard the last of this.'

'And every word a cliché, too,' she murmured with contempt.

'Was that wise? This situation could be misunderstood,' Josh pointed out uneasily.

Ashley had only met Pietro briefly at the wedding. The only child of Vito's elder sister, who was a widow, he bore all the marks of a self-indulgent, adoring mother and too much money. She had known that her marriage to Vito had shattered him. When he had taunted Tim, he had certainly not envisaged Tim's sister becoming his uncle's wife, and he disliked her thoroughly for that piece of apparent one-upmanship.

'Looking scared would only encourage him.' She glanced anxiously at her watch. 'I should be going.'

Vito was striding through the hall when she returned home. She paled like a thief caught with her hand trapped in the till. 'You weren't due back until tomorrow!'

'Should I look under the bed? Search the cupboards?' he teased.

Huddled inside her coat with her stomach sucked in, she looked at him blankly.

'For your lover,' he supplied rather drily. 'It was supposed to be a joke.'

Amusement failed her. As he searched her face, his dark features set hard, making him look tired, irritable.

'"Welcome home, *caro*. I've missed you so much,"' he breathed with glancing satire in a high-pitched treble.

She flushed, her shoulders drooping under the weight of her depression. 'I'm sorry.'

'The last thing I need right now is an apology. *Dio*, what am I? Your gaoler, that you need to cringe when you see me?' he murmured in a fierce undertone.

The burden of her own secrecy constrained her. And what would he have done had she thrown herself into his arms? Such a demonstration would scarcely have been welcome when he no longer found her desirable. The passion had burnt out just as she had known it would, and when he wouldn't even argue with her she knew their relationship was on the rocks. Either that or he was sickening for something, she reflected morosely as she sat down in the palatial drawing-room.

'Mr Angeli, madam.'

Ashley glanced up from her magazine with a frown. Who? Their staff didn't normally show a visitor in until they had established that the visitor was welcome...with one notable exception. Family members. And there, smirking like a cartoon baddie in a comic strip, stood Pietro.

'Vito's upstairs if you want him.' She decided to call his bluff, every muscle in her slight body drawn unnaturally tense.

Pietro strolled over to her. 'You must think I'm stupid. He's in Milan.'

Ashley edged upright uneasily. 'He's upstairs.'

He laughed. 'You wish!'

'Are you threatening me?' she enquired in disbelief.

He drew out a cigarette and lit it with a flourish. 'What do you think?'

'I'd prefer you not to smoke,' she said quietly.

His dark eyes rested on her flatly. He was a very handsome boy, but there was something frighteningly unboyish about the cool way in which he looked her over, as if she was a piece of female flesh on a slab. 'If you think I'm about to listen to some cheap little tart telling me what I can and can't do in my uncle's house, you're even dumber than you look.'

'I'd like you to leave, Pietro.' She drew in a deep, shaky breath.

'I don't think so. You've got it made here, haven't you? I'd hate to rock the newly married boat,' he mocked. 'And I could, believe me. Giulia tells me he's very jealous...nearly made a scene at the engagement party. I can't imagine it myself. I always saw my uncle as a very astute guy, more into banking than bonking——'

'Get out!' she demanded unsteadily.

'You're as over-sensitive as your little twerp of a brother. I did for him nicely, didn't I?' He gave her a self-satisfied smile. 'My friends gave him a right going over, taught him quite a lesson. You should learn from his mistakes. I think you're going to be very nice to me indeed in the near future.'

Ashley was feeling physically sick. Pietro was a teenager like Tim, just a kid, she had to keep on telling herself. But that he should crow about having had her brother beaten up really shook her.

'So do I tell Uncle Vito that I saw you holding hands and weeping over the good doctor this lunchtime or do I keep quiet?' he taunted.

'You tell him whatever you see fit,' she dared.

Pietro grimaced. 'But you see, once I start talking, I might get carried away. I might tell him about the money you took to dump him the last time——'

'What?' she interrupted hoarsely, unable to believe her ears.

'My mother told me about it. It's an open secret in the family,' he shared, enjoying her shock. 'You got a big fat cheque and he got Carina as a consolation prize.'

'I never cashed that cheque!' Ashley gasped, her head reeling.

'Uncle Vito's got a lot of pride...I don't think he's going to be too happy to find out he was dumped for a price——'

'You repulsive little swine!' Ashley suddenly erupted, shuddering with the force of her distaste. 'Have you any idea of how much you could hurt your own grandmother? The damage you could do to her relationship with Vito?'

He called her something foul.

What happened next was a blur. Sick and dizzy, Ashley staggered, feeling the darkness threaten to fold in. She made it back down on to the sofa just as Pietro let out a strangled yell. When she raised her swimming head, she couldn't believe what she was seeing. Vito had his nephew pinned up against the wall with one powerful hand and he was spitting at him in staccato Italian. Uncontrollable rage was the only possible description for the mood her husband was in. He was shaking Pietro as a terrier shook a rat before it went for the jugular.

In sudden alarm, Ashley leapt upright. 'You're hurting him, Vito!'

Her use of English caused Vito to switch to the same language. 'You dare to enter my home and threaten my pregnant wife?' he was roaring. 'When I am finished with you, you will wish you were dead!'

Ashley rather thought he might be, but on the brink of interference she fell back, the paralysis of deeper shock sinking in. Vito had said 'my pregnant wife'. A humming noise interfered with her eardrums. Without the smallest of warnings, she keeled over in a dead faint.

CHAPTER TEN

WHEN Ashley came round, she was lying on her bed. In a flash, everything came back. Vito knew she was pregnant. All her ridiculous precautions had been a complete waste of time. In addition, she now knew why he had changed towards her. At the back of her mind, she had feared the cause had been that last row when she had raved at him like a madwoman. Now she knew differently.

'How do you feel?' Vito enquired with an anxious tremor in the normally level tenor of his voice. 'Should I call a doctor?'

She refused to open her eyes. 'No, that would be making a fuss.'

Vito sighed. 'I'm afraid I have already made a fuss. I've called the family doctor out.'

'Then why did you bother asking me?'

'I was hoping for a sensible answer,' he admitted heavily. 'You know that I know now——'

'How?'

'That last night in Sri Lanka ... I overheard your conversation with Priya.'

Her lashes flew up, revealing incredulous green. 'You didn't look as if you'd overheard!' she protested.

Gracefully he shrugged a shoulder. 'The ability not to betray emotion is useful in the banking world.'

She flinched, turned her head away. 'You should have told me. I feel a fool——'

He released his breath. 'I did hope that you would tell me freely if I gave you time. I was also very surprised,' he confessed quietly. 'Was it that nigh——'

'Yes!' she whipped the word at him to shut him up on a painful subject.

159

'You won't believe me, but I really am sorry——'

'You're right... I don't!'

'You weren't ready for this. It was badly timed,' he murmured tautly.

'My pregnancies usually are. I'm astonished that you're not over the moon!'

'Am I allowed to be?'

She said nothing, drained of response. She stared at the wall. His behaviour since they had returned to London was understandable now. He had been conserving her energies for the baby. Nothing but peace, quiet and tranquillity for the baby's benefit. Nothing else mattered, obviously.

'You've got what you want, so leave me alone,' she mumbled bitterly.

'Do you really think that this is what I want?'

His only answer was her defensively turned back.

'If you hadn't fainted, I might have throttled my nephew,' he remarked, trying a new tack.

'He wouldn't be much of a loss.'

'I was about to enter the room when I heard something that he was saying. I waited until I heard it all,' he delivered. 'And if I don't sound quite myself, it could be because I've had a number of severe shocks this afternoon.'

She worried at her lower lip with her teeth. Exactly how much had he heard? Slowly she turned over again. Vito was standing by the window, tall, dark and very still. He was emanating turmoil in waves though. The atmosphere was crackling with tension.

'It would appear that Pietro lied to me about his dealings with your brother——'

'My delinquent, violent brother?'

Vito flinched, and, annoyingly, the sight gave her no satisfaction. Instead she found herself wanting to offer comfort. Vito was one of those people who very rarely found themselves in the wrong. A perfectionist with a strong sense of fair play, he now found himself in a most invidious position. Tim had certainly not deserved a prison sentence for losing his head. Tim had been most brutally provoked—Ashley was sure of that after what she herself had undergone at Pietro's hands. And Tim hadn't even told her about the accusation concerning the money she had supposedly taken. Tim had known it for a lie. But did Vito?

'I misjudged him as badly as I misjudged my nephew. My only excuse is that I have had very little contact with Pietro in recent years and until I actually heard him speaking to you I would have continued to defend him because... because he is family.' He made the admission through bloodlessly compressed lips. 'Since his father died, we have all spoilt him, indulged him, self-evidently ruined his character...'

'Oh, stop blaming yourself,' Ashley groaned. 'He's a conceited, nasty, vicious little creep. Any family as large as yours is bound to have at least one revolting specimen.'

'I very much regret that both you and your brother should have had to suffer at his hands——'

'I've suffered more at yours.'

As quickly as she said it, she regretted it. She didn't know him in this mood. He was under great strain. His stance, his clenched features and pallor told her that. But he was also still very much in control. There was iron in Vito's soul. A lesser man might have buckled beneath the revelations he had had to endure. But not Vito. He was ashamed of his nephew's behaviour. He felt it as a personal slight. However, he was not about to set her free in restitution. Not now that she was pregnant, she acknowledged painfully.

'Is it true that my mother gave you money?'

The iron control was under threat now. She sat up, meeting the savage darkness of his challenging gaze and she knew that he very much wanted to hear that Pietro had been talking rubbish. 'She came to see me the day before you asked me to marry you——'

His even white teeth gritted in a flash against his dark skin. 'And she offered you money to get out of my life?'

Ashley bent her head. 'No, she wasn't as crude as that. She put the cheque on the table as she left. I expect she thought you were keeping me and she didn't want me to——' She winced as he said a very rude word in Italian. 'That's all there really is to it.'

'If you don't tell me, I'll get it out of her,' he spelt out icily, but his tone belied the smouldering anger of humiliation in his hard stare. 'I want to know exactly what was said.'

Ashley didn't have the energy for a struggle with the sheer overwhelming force of Vito's will. 'What do you think?' she muttered dully. 'That I wouldn't be able to fit, that I wouldn't be able to cope, that I'd embarrass you. I didn't have the right background, the right religion, the right anything. In short, I would ruin your life.'

His back was turned to her, the defensive bunching of his muscles visible even through his well-cut jacket. Without warning, he struck the wall with a coiled fist, making her flinch. 'She was wrong,' he whispered, savagely sardonic. 'I didn't need you to ruin my life. Then and now, I was perfectly capable of doing that for myself.'

'She did it with the best of intentions. She didn't know me. She must have been worried about your father——'

'I'll never forgive her,' Vito swore violently. 'I was no helpless teenager in need of her protection!'

'A son is always a son no matter what age he is.'

'You defend her?' He surveyed her with complete incredulity. 'Why?'

Ashley sighed. 'I think she saved us from making a bad mistake.'

Harsh lines indented the curve between his nose and mouth. He was rigid, palpably restraining the rawness of his emotions with the thinnest remaining edge of control. 'What a shame that she couldn't whisk you out of harm's way this time. It seems that she would have done both of us a very big favour.'

Ashley turned white as though he had struck her, and in a way he might as well have done, so complete was that bitter force of his rejection. She bowed her head, closed her eyes, struggling to absorb the immensity of her pain and conceal it from him.

The doctor's arrival was a welcome interruption. He walked into an atmosphere that could have been cut with a knife. Complete rest and calm and no upsets was his practical prescription. Dinner was brought to her on a tray. She napped for a while after she had eaten, having given up waiting for Vito to reappear.

Much later she opened her sleepy eyes on lamplight. Vito was casting a long shadow by the window. He wore neither tie nor jacket. With his black hair tousled and his jawline darkly shadowed, he failed his usual standards of perfect grooming. He also had a glass in his hand.

'What time is it?' she muttered.

'Midnight...later.' With an infinitesimal shrug, he sighed. 'I really don't know.' The syllables dragged ever so slightly.

That very faint slur betrayed him. His mother was right all along, she decided. I'm the kiss of death to Vito...I'm driving him to drink.

He cleared his throat. 'I've seen Lorena, Pietro's mother. She knows now what he has done. She intends to return to Italy with him. She is very close to her late husband's family and believes that they will help her to exercise greater control over his son. I am not so optimistic. I suspect that Pietro will remain a problem.'

Ashley surfaced from the bedding with the sensual glide of a mermaid emerging from the waves. She sat up, righting the slipping satin strap of her diaphanous nightdress. 'You've had a busy evening,' she said, combing her fingers slowly through her vibrant mane of hair so that it fell in a silken mass across her pale shoulders. It was so much wasted effort. The male who would have been electrified by such a display a mere fortnight ago still didn't spare her a glance. 'I'm feeling much better,' she added.

'Good.' The tone was strained. He stared moodily down into the crystal glass he held. 'I seem to have this extraordinary talent for destroying what you hold dear. Yet you must accept that I never intended, never planned for it to be that way. I thought I had the right...I thought that you owed me this chance——'

Unbearably taut, she whispered, 'I'm not sure I follow.'

He threw back his head and laughed with savage amusement. Her entire attention was fiercely locked to him, her heartbeat racing even in that moment of stress to the raw, virile power of his male beauty. 'I have never been afflicted by any great degree of humility,' he confided shamelessly. 'You see, I thought that I could make you love me...'

A hoarse sound of distress escaped her. A shudder of reaction forced a passage through her tense body. He confirmed her own suspicions but it had been many weeks since she had dwelt on those suspicions which would have clouded and ruined that final, glorious month in Sri Lanka.

'I actually thought that if I pushed all the right buttons, it would happen. You would wake up one day and, far from wanting to stick a knife between my ribs,' he asserted harshly, 'you would think, I cannot live without this guy. And you would cling like ivy, cleave like Eve to Adam in the Bible——'

'I think I get the picture, Vito.' It took her a full thirty seconds to even make her voice work and it emerged rusty and flat, unable to rise above the tremendous pain she was fighting to hide. No wonder he had decided not to get her pregnant. He had been far more intent on revenge and he had gone to a lot of effort...in fact he had gone to the most unbelievable lengths to push what he had called 'the right buttons'. And had she been honest with him, he might have been spared all that tedious exertion. He had actually got what he wanted far more quickly and easily than he could ever have guessed. She was so desperately hurt, so horribly humiliated that she wanted to die.

He released his breath in a hiss. 'I was incredibly conceited——'

'Yes.' And with just cause, she conceded wretchedly. She had been a vulnerable target, a willing victim.

'To even think that after all that I had done to you, you could even...even begin to care for me again,' he practically muttered, sounding rather peculiar.

Since she hadn't brought herself to look once at him in the last few minutes, she presumed it was the effect of the alcohol. 'C-crazy,' she managed jerkily half under her breath.

'It was unforgivable.'

Dumbly she nodded agreement.

'Manipulative, calculating,' he breathed raggedly, an edge of something remarkably similar to desperation in his delivery. 'I can't help being like that...'

She knew what he wanted. He wanted her to shout at him and throw in a few adjectives of her own. It would make him feel better. But for the first time in her life with Vito, she had absolutely nothing to say. Her defences were down. She was in too much pain to feel anger. He would just have to live with his conscience.

'I can't bear your silence,' he admitted gruffly.

Accidentally, she glanced up and collided with lustrous dark eyes. He looked shattered, as if every sentence he had spoken had taken a physical toll. She had never seen him like that before: vulnerable, unsure. No doubt she would never see him like that again. He had plunged them both into an unholy mess but she had every certainty that by tomorrow Vito would be concentrating his immense energy and brilliant mind on how to approach with tact the problem of the custody of her unborn children. Two for the price of one and he didn't even know it yet, she reflected mirthlessly.

'Perhaps you would prefer to talk tomorrow when we are both feeling calmer...'

She never wanted to talk to him again, but she nodded and went back to studying the sheet she was nervously pleating. There was no way she could sleep after he had gone. Could he take her children away from her? She hadn't signed anything. She wasn't a drug addict or an alcoholic. She couldn't see what possible argument he could put up in a court of law... Some time around dawn, she fell into an uneasy doze.

'You don't feel car-sick?' Vito shot her a concerned glance.

Ashley's teeth clenched. That was the third time he had referred to her health. Add that litany to three other stilted remarks ranging from the weather to the beauty of the countryside and you had a far from scintillating dialogue.

She had spent yesterday in bed. She had got up for breakfast and he had mentioned talking as in proper talking and she had suffered a sudden relapse, pleading weakness to escape. When had he turned her into such a coward? They couldn't live in limbo forever. Either she talked or she ran away, and if she ran away she would be running to the end of her days, despising herself for such cowardice.

Just about the last thing she had expected this morning was the announcement that they had a luncheon engagement in deepest Berkshire and that he had no intention of making excuses for her absence. With bad grace she had surrendered, marvelling that he could think a lunch date worthy of such attention in the present state of their marriage.

'I want us to stay together.'

The cool assertion dropped like a brick through the windscreen, momentarily depriving her of breath.

'Until the baby is born,' he added very quietly. 'That is very important to me.'

'Tough!' Biting her lip until the blood came, she stared out at the motorway stretching endlessly ahead and thought that he had chosen his time well. There was nowhere to run. Stay until the baby is born and then get lost. She felt sick, horribly sick, shrinking from the mere suggestion. Didn't he have any sensitivity at all? To continue to live with him would destroy her. She needed to get away to get over him. She needed to go back to her own world, away from his and every reminder of him. But the leaving would be hard because incredibly, even after all he had done, a shameful part of her still wanted to cling to what little of a semblance of a marriage remained.

'The last time I wasn't there——'

'I don't need you!' she spat jerkily. 'I don't need you for anything.'

'I didn't say that you did.' He was measuring his words with supreme tact. 'But I would like you to stay——'

'So that you can watch over me?' she cut in bitterly. 'Make sure I don't sneak off for another termination?'

The lean brown fingers on the steering-wheel clenched to show white knuckles. 'You didn't have one the first time. Why should you want one now?'

Ashley was shaken. He was telling her that he believed her, he believed that she had had a miscarriage four years ago. 'When did you change your mind and decide that I wasn't lying?'

'Weeks ago, but you didn't want to talk about it,' he reminded her drily.

'I didn't see why I should have to keep on defending myself.'

'I really do want this baby,' he breathed almost roughly. 'I may have failed you in the past but that does not mean I have absolutely no rights this time.'

'I don't want to talk about your rights,' she whispered sickly.

'Why the hell have you never learned to speak my language?' he suddenly raked at her furiously. 'It is not easy for me to find the correct words to express my emotions in English. What do you think this is like for me? I am in the wrong! In every direction I look, I am even more in the wrong! If I spent the rest of my life telling you that I was sorry, it wouldn't change anything!'

'Five minutes of you saying sorry in any language would be a wonder to me. Let's not go overboard by talking about the rest of your life!'

'I'm getting off this motorway,' he gritted.

'Not one of your brighter ideas,' she said dulcetly, unable to stop stabbing at him. A row about nothing in particular was much more her style than a discussion about the burial arrangements for their marriage. 'And if you don't stop speeding we will probably be greeted with a roadblock at the next exit.'

He took the next exit in smouldering, simmering silence and shot into a lay-by five minutes later, killing the engine-purr with a suddenness that brought the silence rushing dangerously back.

'I'm sorry... is that what you want?'

Green eyes flashing, she dealt him a taut look of mutiny and turned her head deliberately to stare out of the side-window. He could never be sorry enough. Two and a half months ago she had been reasonably happy, hating him, and right now she was sickeningly miserable loving him for no return. So he wanted the baby. Well, that was scarcely news. 'Do you feel sick'? 'Do you feel faint'? 'Do you want to stop for coffee'? The message of his concern for the life in her womb had been beaten in with overkill.

'I'm sorry if I forced you to marry me. I'm sorry I threatened your brother. I'm sorry I got you pregnant,' he unleashed raggedly. 'Does that make you feel better?'

'Not so that you'd notice.' Her lips were compressed in a white line. She was terrified that she would burst into tears. Her hormones were sloshing about, threatening a scene. She really didn't want to hear how much he regretted getting her pregnant. That assurance merely underlined how eager he would have been to get rid of her had she not proved to be so distressingly fertile.

With a stifled curse, he reached out and tried to grasp her hand, but her fingers were clenched into a fist that had no welcome. He withdrew his hand, released his seatbelt and turned round. 'I care about what happens to you.'

'If you say anything more as nauseating,' she gasped, 'I'll be sick!'

Searching her white, shuttered face, he evidently registered that that was not mere dramatics. He leant back in his seat, palpably putting a lid on his frustration. Silence stretched and gnawed at her nerves.

'I can't change what happened between us four years ago!' he grated abruptly. 'You failed your exams. Your family turned their back on you. I married another woman and you lost the baby. I wasn't there and I should have been. I feel bloody guilty——'

'It won't last,' she said flippantly, masking her distress.

'It doesn't cost you anything to let me speak,' Vito responded harshly. 'I let you down badly. I accept that.' All of a sudden he was talking in jerky snatches and the silence came back for an entire minute before he breathed, 'I am deeply ashamed of my own behaviour. I took the easy way out. You hurt me and I walked away.'

'Don't forget the cheque-book.' As soon as she said it, she wished she hadn't. It had been below the belt. All these admissions of guilt, shame and regret were costing him blood. Vito was very proud, very confident of his own judgement. For the first time in his magnificently successful existence, Vito was forcing himself to acknowledge mistakes openly. Unfortunately she didn't want his guilt any more than she wanted his apologies. Neither was capable of healing her own pain. He didn't love her, and right now she hated him for it.

He ignored the unforgiving dig but he was very pale beneath his golden skin, taut as a drawn bow. 'I didn't know that I had the power to hurt you then. I didn't understand you. I was afraid of losing you. I resented everything you put before me. The more freedom you demanded, the more angry I became. Sometimes...sometimes I hated you almost as much as I loved you——'

Accidentally she collided with brilliant dark eyes in an instant of perfect mutual understanding. She glanced away again instantly.

'You made me feel insecure, and nobody had ever made me feel like that before...'

She was astonished, green eyes flying to him involuntarily. His sensual mouth had a grim, bitter twist as he gazed fearlessly back at her. 'You were far too young for me.'

'Yes,' she conceded unsteadily. 'I didn't understand what I was doing. I was trying to protect myself. I didn't want to be hurt. I didn't want to love you. I didn't want you to get the upper hand.'

'I didn't,' he murmured with dark satire.

But he had. He had. His life had gone on afterwards. Hers had stopped dead. It hadn't been worth it, none of her proud defences had been worth it four years ago. In one sense she had driven him away, had brought about her own downfall. Had he known that she loved him, he would have trusted her more than he had and that day he wouldn't have sat in the car instead of crossing the street to speak to her.

'I phoned you...I phoned you in Italy,' she told him in a rush. 'I was going to tell you about the baby——'

His ebony brows drew together. 'I received no call——'

'Giulia came to the phone. She said you were in the middle of your engagement party...I didn't say anything,' Ashley confessed starkly. 'There really wasn't anything to say.'

He groaned something in Italian but he said nothing in his own defence. His dark features broodingly tense, he avoided meeting her eyes, but a surge of blood lay like a betraying line across his blunt cheekbones. He started up the car again. 'It's getting late,' he said flatly.

'Can't we forget about lunch?' she enquired hopefully. 'Phone and make an excuse?'

He tensed. 'No.'

'I don't feel like socialising.'

'It's out of the question. We have to show,' he asserted wryly.

Half an hour later, she was dredged from the all-consuming energy of her thoughts by the strange realisation that the car was passing familiar landmarks. They were within ten miles of her family home, she registered uncomfortably.

'Where do these people live?' she asked stiffly.

'Not far from here.'

'I grew up around here,' she divulged reluctantly. 'You could be more precise.'

'You can give me directions when we reach your home town.'

Ashley stopped breathing. 'Is that where they live?' she demanded.

Vito cast her a rueful glance and sighed. 'I'm taking you home, *cara*.'

She froze in shock. 'I don't believe you!'

'I phoned your mother yesterday and she invited us down to lunch——'

'Stop the car!' Ashley gasped. 'I'm not going!'

'Yes, you are,' Vito contradicted flatly. 'And you're going to mend fences. It's my fault that you're at odds with your family. This is the one thing that I can do for you——'

'Do for me?' she echoed, on the edge of hysteria.

Completely misunderstanding the source of her distress, Vito dealt her a soothing but arrogant smile. 'They won't reject you. Your mother can't wait to see you. She was in tears on the phone.'

Ashley could believe that, but she was equally well aware that her mother had made not the slightest effort to see her in recent years. Sylvia Forrester had abided obediently by her husband's rules, so why on earth was she inviting them to lunch? Was it possible that time had softened her father? She wanted to believe that so much it hurt. She had missed her mother desperately, would have long since arrived up on the doorstep of her own volition had she not been conscious that such defiance would only cause more trouble for her mother.

'My father hates me,' she confided tightly.

'Fathers don't hate their children. My father would have been equally outraged if one of my sisters had lived with a man outside marriage. The situation is quite different now that we are married, and tempers will have cooled long ago,' he drawled with complete conviction.

He didn't understand, and already they were driving through the town. He didn't need her directions. Staverston wasn't that big and her father's car showroom dominated the end of the main street. Her home was only fifty yards beyond, set back from the road, an Edwardian detached behind a low brick wall.

Climbing out of the car, Vito scanned her paralysed stillness. 'Come on,' he urged.

Susan answered the doorbell, looking pale and tense. Vito introduced himself with immense calm. 'We're out in the garden,' she said uncomfortably. 'Mum invited us down. I hope you don't mind.'

'The more, the merrier,' Ashley quipped. 'Tim?'

'He's in Greece with his friends. Dad's treat.'

Ashley moved towards the French windows which led out to the garden and abruptly Susan barred her path, embarrassment and anxiety mingling in her gaze. 'Dad doesn't know you're coming,' she shared in a tremulous rush. 'I can't believe Mum's doing this——'

Before Ashley could respond, her father's harsh voice sounded forth from the kitchen. 'You utterly stupid woman!' he was thundering in a well-remembered tone that brought Ashley out in a cold sweat. 'I'm not going to eat foreign muck like that! All this palaver for that gutless fool Arnold? How dare you waste my money on...?'

For a timeless moment of horror the three of them were a frozen tableau. Ashley could hear her mother's voice raised in a hideously familiar whine of apology and placation. Her stomach turned over sickly.

'Do come out into the garden,' Susan said almost pleadingly to Vito.

Ashley was cringing with humiliation, unable to look at Vito, her cheeks as scarlet as her sister's. Vito would have to draw on every ounce of his well-bred *savoir-faire* to get through even a brief meeting with her father. She was unnerved by the prospect of the coming scene and devastated by the news that her mother had invited them without her father's permission.

Beyond the French windows, she watched her father's stocky but broadly built figure powering angrily out to the patio where Arnold was sitting reading a newspaper. Her hand touched Vito's, staying him. 'I think I'd better do this on my own,' she said tautly.

'Good idea,' Susan cut in brightly. 'Let me get you a drink, Vito.'

Ashley crossed the patio. Her father was telling Arnold that only wimps played golf and Arnold was calmly agreeing with him, impervious to the insult intended. A quiet, unaggressive man, Arnold flatly refused to be drawn into disputes with his difficult father-in-law.

'Dad...' Her voice wavered as she fell still in the sunlight, her shoulders back, her chin raised high.

Hunt Forrester rose like an angry bull at a gate, his full face set in lines of disbelief. 'What the hell are *you* doing here?'

Ashley forced herself forward. 'D-don't you think it's time we made peace?'

'You shameless little bitch, how dare you show your face here?' he roared, striding over to grip her by the shoulders. 'I told you never to come back, didn't I? You don't belong to this family any more! You never did, you little slut! But you can't leave us alone, can you? You damn near put Tim in prison with your shenanigans——'

'Dad, please...' His fingers were biting like steel pincers into her shrinking flesh. With every spitting syllable he was giving her a violent shake to punctuate his fury.

'Release my wife.' Vito's intervention carried at least ten generations of aristocratic cool and disdain.

'Stay out of this, Vito!' Ashley cried fearfully.

'Or you might get hurt,' Hunt Forrester sneered, sizing up the younger man's superbly well-cut suit and silk shirt, his contempt blatant.

'Your daughter is pregnant,' Vito delivered icily.

Ashley was dizzy and sick. Somewhere in the background she could hear her mother quietly sobbing. It was all so horribly familiar but for the first time she realised that she didn't need to be afraid of her father. Vito would not allow him to harm her.

'So that's how you got him to the altar!' her father gibed hatefully. 'Second time lucky, it seems——'

Pressing her back with one formidable hand, Vito hit her father so hard that he went flying back on to the lawn. Susan screamed. Arnold flew upright. Ashley sagged back in shock against the table, her knees too wobbly to hold her.

'If you want a fight,' Vito was snarling, 'pick on someone more your own size!'

CHAPTER ELEVEN

ARNOLD socked a clenched fist into his palm, his normally serious features alive with pleasure. 'That was some punch!' he crowed, shaking his head in admiration.

'At least you've more gumption than that idiot behind me!' Hunt growled as he picked himself up. 'But you can take your wife and get out——'

'If they go, I go!' The tremulous threat turned all their heads. Sylvia Forrester looked in despair at her younger daughter. 'Could I stay with you for a while?'

'What...what the devil's going on here?' Hunt ejaculated incredulously. 'Have you gone out of your mind, Sylvie?'

'I should have done it years ago...didn't have the guts.' Sylvia extended a shaking hand to Ashley. 'But when I couldn't go to my own child's wedding...I realised how terribly weak I'd become. I'm so sorry I let him do this to you.'

'You're very welcome in our home, Mrs Forrester,' Vito said gently.

'Now just a minute here——' Ashley's father blustered.

'Call me Sylvia,' her mother said shyly. 'You're very kind——'

'He bloody hit me!' Hunt thundered in disbelief.

'And you deserved it.' Trembling in spite of Ashley's supportive arm, Sylvia murmured, 'I'm going to tell her why you treat her the way you do. She has the right to know.'

'No!' Hunt roared.

'Let's go indoors,' Vito suggested.

In bewilderment, Ashley glanced back to where her father was left standing alone. Her head was swimming.

175

She had not thought it possible that her mother could take such a stance against her father. Nor could she even begin to imagine what Sylvia could possibly have to tell her that could upset her father to such an extent.

'Susan, I think you and Arnold should go home,' her mother sighed. 'I'll phone you later.'

As her sister and her husband left the room with pronounced reluctance, her father appeared in the doorway. 'Please don't tell them,' he gritted. 'It's none of their business.'

'You made it Ashley's business.' Her mother lifted her tear-streaked face up. 'Everybody's suffered for my mistake. You should have divorced me. Instead you've taken it out on all of us for over twenty years.'

'Sylvie——' Hunt looked grey, strangely shrunken in stature.

'I—I had an affair.' Sylvia stumbled over the admission, didn't meet anyone's eyes. 'And your father found out. When I discovered that I was pregnant, I . . . I wasn't sure that it was your father's child——'

'Oh, dear God——' Ashley collapsed down into the nearest chair, absolutely devastated by what she believed was coming.

Quietly her mother was crying. 'Your father knew . . . and wh-when you were born with all that red hair, so different-looking from Susan . . . you see, we both assumed that you *couldn't* be his child and I was so ashamed . . . so grateful that your father was prepared to bring you up as his.'

But he hadn't been able to meet that challenge, Ashley completed strickenly. She was appalled by what her mother had revealed.

'I believe that Ashley misunderstands,' Vito murmured. 'You cannot be telling her that she is not her father's child. Tim and Ashley could pass for twins.'

'The other m-man had sandy hair,' her mother whispered unsteadily. 'We forgot that my grandmother had been auburn-haired. It wasn't until Tim was born six years later that we realised that we'd made a mistake, and by then the damage to Ashley's relationship with her father was already done. He still behaved as though she wasn't his... I think that every time he looked at her he remembered that other man.'

The silence went on forever. Ashley's father was hunched in a chair, his spread hands covering his face. He looked like a man on whom a sentence of death had been pronounced. Ashley was in a complete daze. Unconsciously she focused on Vito for what to do or say next. Her heart had gone out to her mother but a second later she experienced an astonishing pang of pity for her father. Her mother's confession had broken him by depriving him of all dignity. Yet Ashley had learnt much more. Her father must have loved her mother a great deal not to divorce her. But unhappily he had been punishing her ever since.

'Do you still want to leave with us?' Vito asked her mother calmly. Ashley repressed an almost hysterical giggle. Trust Vito to stay in control when the rest of them were all falling apart at the seams in front of him.

There was a long silence.

'I—I think that Hunt and I have a lot to discuss,' Sylvia said hesitantly. She stood up with an air of fledgeling confidence and control that shook her daughter. There was a new strength in her mother's stature.

'We'll get lunch at a hotel.' With complete cool, Vito whisked Ashley out to the hall.

Sylvia engulfed her daughter in an emotional embrace. 'I'm so sorry, but I can't leave your father when he's like this.'

'She won't leave him,' Vito asserted as they drove off. 'He's gone to pieces. I think that little scene just cleared the air for them both. The truth needed to come out. It's a shame it didn't happen sooner for your benefit.'

Ashley stole a glance at him. His hard-edged profile was fiercely clenched, the skin pulled tight over his angular cheekbones. She had been wrong to believe that the episode had not affected him, although she could

not really understand why he should look so shattered.
For he did. Pale and shattered.

'Tell me what it was like growing up with a father like
that? With a mother who didn't stand up for you and
a brother-in-law who evidently chose to stand on the
sidelines as well?'

Her hands were shaking. She couldn't find any of her
flippant responses. She was still too disturbed by what
had occurred. 'Scary,' she confided jerkily. 'Lonely.'

Vito vented a harsh expletive.

'Everybody suffered,' she extended. 'I think Tim got
away the lightest because he was a boy and Dad's
favourite. Susan married Arnold to escape. There was
so much tension ... so many arguments. I always fought
him. Looking back, it seems so stupid but he picked on
me.' And all of a sudden something that she had never
ever talked about was finding its own voice and the
memories were spilling out of her almost faster than she
could frame the words to describe them. The constant
criticism and belittling. The sarcasm and the punish-
ments. The fact that her mother had often paid the price
for her defiance. The guilt. The shame that her father
could find her so unworthy of attention or affection.

'You still haven't told me that he hit you, and he did,'
Vito countered darkly. 'I saw it in his face and yours. I
wanted to keep on hitting him. It would have given me
immense satisfaction.'

'Don't! He didn't really hit me,' she protested. 'Not
the way you read about but ... but I was always afraid
that he would because he got so angry with me.' Uneasily
she swallowed, suppressing those memories.

'No wonder you wanted your freedom at university.
You had never had any before.' The flat syllables were
curiously clipped.

'No.' She was glad that he understood.

He asked her if she was hungry. Her stomach rebelled
at the mere thought of food. Once or twice she tried to
initiate conversation but Vito had become disturbingly
uncommunicative. But then, he had just met the in-laws

from hell, she reflected in strong chagrin. Yet she felt curiously at peace. Questions that had troubled her for much of her childhood had been answered. She was not in herself so repulsive that her father couldn't love her. No, she had become the innocent victim of her mother's affair, the focus of all her father's bitterness.

They separated when they got home. Vito said he had some calls to make.

'I'll order a late lunch,' she said.

'I'm not hungry.' The harsh edge to his response made her tense. She wondered what on earth was wrong. His darkly handsome features were shuttered by a fierce constraint beyond her comprehension. But before she could speak he was taking the stairs two at a time.

An hour later she went in search of him. Their chauffeur passed by her on the stairs, carrying two cases. With a frown, Ashley walked into Vito's bedroom suite. He was standing at the window like someone in a trance, blistering tension emanating from him in waves.

'I didn't know you had another trip,' she murmured tightly. 'You didn't mention it.'

Vito swung round. 'I'm returning to Italy. I can't stay here.'

'You're leaving?' White as a sheet from the sheer shock of his sudden change of heart, Ashley simply stared at him. 'But you said——'

'That I wanted to stay until the baby was born,' he completed. 'But we both know that that isn't what you want.'

She locked her hands together before they could betray her by shaking. Her fingers twisted into each other. 'I don't understand.'

Vito released his breath jerkily, his dark eyes locked to her. 'I think it's past time that I stopped knocking my head up against a brick wall and simply took account of your wishes for a change.'

Only hours ago he had been fighting with her to convince her that he should stay. She just couldn't believe that he now wanted out . . . without warning . . . without discussion...without anything. 'But I didn't say that I wanted you to leave——'

'You don't need to. I know how you feel about me,' he asserted almost thickly, his strong bone-structure prominent with strain beneath his golden skin. 'To persist in the face of such odds would be utter insanity. I'm not blaming you. Considering what I've done...' He faltered and sucked in air, shifted an expressive hand. 'Well, you've been very tolerant, much more tolerant than I had any right to expect in the circumstances. But I have to face facts. You would be a lot more comfortable if I weren't here——'

'If you're trying to convince me that you're doing this for my benefit rather than your own, you're not getting anywhere!' Ashley threw at him in a shaken undertone, crossing her arms over her breasts as if she needed that support.

'Hennessy will be happier if I'm not around and so will I be,' Vito admitted with sudden stark force.

'What has Josh got to do with this?'

'*Madre di Dio*!' Vito swore rawly, swinging away from her again. 'You're involved with him and I am the intruder, not he, since I forced you into this marriage. Clearly he was on the scene at the time and I could hardly expect you to admit the fact. Now you will be free to continue your liaison——'

Did his conscience require the sop that she had another man waiting for her? Dear God, she had totally forgotten that Vito had heard Pietro referring to her holding hands and weeping over Josh that day. There had been so much else happening, it had completely slipped her mind. She looked at Vito, rigid, brooding and unbelievably tense, not exactly the last of the liberated husbands in her own opinion. And here he was, giving her *carte blanche* to...dear heaven, how dared he?

'I haven't the slightest intention of becoming involved with Josh,' she snapped out. 'Unlike you, I don't flit like a butterfly from one person to another.'

'I didn't flit to Carina's arms,' Vito bit out with lancing bitterness. 'I fell into them in a drunken, mindless stupor!'

Ashley stilled. 'I beg your pardon?'

'It's really not important——'

'It is to me!'

Reluctantly he turned back to her. 'I considered her to be a close friend,' he confided. 'And one evening, not very long after I had learnt of your visit to that clinic, I went to her apartment...'

'And?' Ashley prompted fiercely.

'I needed someone to talk to but I was very drunk,' he spelt out with distaste, a dark flush of embarrassment accentuating the hard slant of his cheekbones. 'The next morning I woke up in her bed with no memory whatsoever of how I had got there.'

Deeply pained by the image, Ashley turned her head away.

'That's why I married her. She loved me. I believed that I had taken advantage of that. I felt that I had to marry her,' he admitted tautly. 'I thought that you had someone else, I thought that you had had an abortion——'

'Yes,' she conceded strickenly.

'My father was so ill that my mother urged haste. It was complete madness.' Vito emitted a humourless laugh. 'I had lost you. I really didn't care what I did and in that state I married. Only after the wedding did Carina confess that nothing had happened that night. So you see, *cara*...I was an absolute fool. Had my wits been about me, I might have suspected that I was too incapable of a night of passion, but my wits weren't about me.'

He hadn't told her the truth about his marriage to Carina because that truth had made him feel stupid. Carina had trapped him in the only way she could, relying on his sense of honour to close the bars on that trap.

His mouth tightened. 'I should be entirely honest with you. That wasn't the only reason I married her. She loved me and I wanted you to know that I could get on with my life without you. Not quite the best reason for marrying anyone...least of all a woman worthy of more than I was ever able to give her——'

'She made her choice.'

Vito grimaced. 'She knew I didn't love her but she had this sunny belief that in the end I would. *She* put up the photos everywhere. They made me feel guilty... that's why it took me so long to have them put away. It was almost as though she was afraid that I forgot she existed if she wasn't immediately in front of me!'

Ashley winced.

Vito straightened. 'I did try to make her happy, but I failed. I couldn't manufacture love to order. I'm really not very good in relationships...in fact, I'm bloody useless!'

'No, you're not. If she knew that you didn't love her, she must surely have known that there would be problems——'

'Which of us are so practical about attaining our heart's desire?' His lustrous dark eyes clung to her briefly and then he squared his broad shoulders and turned away. 'Four years ago, I was so crazy about you I would have married you the first week we met. That wasn't practical either, was it? And that's why I'm leaving now. I don't want your pity.'

'Why would I pity you?' Ashley demanded in a rush of bitterness. 'You were out for revenge, Vito, and you certainly took it!'

'I never wanted revenge,' Vito contradicted with a harsh laugh. 'I wanted you...I needed you, and within days I knew I was still in love with you!'

Ashley gaped at him, transfixed.

'You wouldn't have given me a second chance if I'd asked for one. You hated me,' he intoned, pale and taut. 'I thought I could make you love me——'

He had said exactly the same thing two days ago in her bedroom, only she had completely misunderstood what he was telling her. He had been telling her that he still loved her, asking if she could ever forgive him for what he had done—and she had made no response. 'I can't bear your silence', he had said.

'But you said you wanted a child!' she cried.

He grimaced. 'I didn't want you to suspect how badly I needed you. And if there was a child, I intended to use that child to keep you. I was betting on a dark horse but I couldn't believe that you would be able to walk away.'

'You were right.'

'One right and countless wrongs,' he countered savagely.

'No,' she countered with a soft catch in her voice. 'Your score is just a little higher. When did you realise that I wasn't lying about having had a miscarriage?'

He flung her an impatient look. 'Does that matter now?'

'Yes,' she insisted, thinking she was a heel to keep him in suspense like this, but she had to know.

'After you had that accident in Sri Lanka. I really thought I had lost you. Such shocks tend to clear the head,' he grated. 'I realised that I loved you and that nothing else past or present mattered. My own obstinacy was the biggest barrier between us. I had to let go of my own bitterness. You had never lied to me, so why—I had to ask myself—should you be lying now, in the present?'

Ashley was trembling with the force of her emotion. 'You'd better unpack again. I don't want you to go.'

He went rigid, slashed a hand through the air. 'But I can't live with you like this! This afternoon, I saw how you must always have seen me,' he delivered half under his breath, his strong emotion palpable. 'I saw what you must truly think of me. You believe that I am a man like your father——'

As she finally understood what had forced his decision to leave, she could have cried. Vito had seen the childhood source of all her defences and put the wrong interpretation on that new knowledge. 'Never,' she argued with determination, not yet ready to admit to him that she had ever been so foolish. 'My father made me afraid of loving. He made me afraid of marriage. He made me afraid of turning out like my mother. Loving you terrified me four years ago! I just couldn't handle it. But I can handle it now. Don't you see that? I don't hate you, Vito... I love you.'

The torment in his intense gaze as he struggled to believe threatened to tear her apart. He crossed the room, reached out two powerful arms and hauled her up against him hard. She met the hot violence of his drugging mouth with equally fierce demands of her own. She couldn't get enough of him. He couldn't get enough of her. Breathing was a challenge as she sunk her greedy fingers into the springy depths of his hair and trapped him in place.

'*Dio*, it's been so long,' he groaned, surfacing for air. 'I would give ten years of my life to make love to you now!'

'No such sacrifice required.' Ashley hauled him back into her arms with unashamed tenacity.

In the act of being dragged towards the bed, he stiffened and dug long fingers into her mane of hair to still their progress. 'We can't,' he sighed. 'The baby. I read this book.'

'Wh-what book?' she stammered, suddenly embarrassed by her own lack of inhibition.

He stared down at her, gravely serious. 'If there's a danger of miscarriage... no sex.'

'My consultant told me that there's no grounds for my worries,' Ashley whispered, quivering in a white heat of excitement as he involuntarily responded to her proximity by grinding his hips against her in a movement of such blatant male need that her brain cells all turned simultaneously to sludge.

'Are you sure?'

Single-mindedly, she ran teasing fingers down the line of his straining zip. As she leant against him, her hand lingered there in an uninhibited hunger of fascination. It was over a fortnight since he had touched her, and, now that she knew why he had practised such restraint, all inhibitions were cast to the four winds. He was incredibly, wonderfully aroused.

'*Dio*, I would die if I lost you again,' he bit out raggedly.

'No chance,' she asserted unsteadily.

'Do you really love me?'

'Passionately...madly...forever,' she gasped under the wild onslaught of his hands and mouth. 'Vito...your chauffeur must be waiting in the car!'

He fell back on the bed with her, deaf to all reasoning of the prosaic variety. 'I can't believe that you can forgive me,' he groaned into her hair. 'I screwed up at every turn.'

'I'll take it out of your hide...my way,' Ashley told him.

He bit sensuously at the ripe curve of her breast as he slowly dispensed with the scrap of lace depriving him of proper access. 'I'm all yours,' he confided. 'My jealousy blinded me to what I was doing to you in the past. I spent four hellish years wanting you. I nearly worked myself to death trying to forget you. And then you walked into my office that day and suddenly I knew that I would move heaven and earth to get you back. That night, after the opera, I knew that I still loved you. I was devastated by how I felt. I wasn't in control——'

'Neither was I, and that's the way it should be.' She ran loving fingers along the taut line of his mouth. 'You brought us together again. How could I not forgive you for that?' she teased.

'I'll never forgive myself for not being there when you lost the baby,' he admitted gruffly.

Her green eyes shadowed. 'I wanted it so much because you had gone. That was all I had left——'

'Don't——' As he buried his face in the sweet valley between her breasts, she felt the moisture on his cheeks, comprehended his sudden rigidity.

She smoothed his head in forgiveness but her own throat was closing over. 'It happens, Vito. It just wasn't meant to be.' And maybe it would be the same this time too, she conceded painfully, but wishing and worrying weren't likely to change her prospects either way. Perhaps tomorrow she would share those fears. But not tonight. Now was a time to celebrate the sheer joy of being together.

But Vito was not so easily diverted. He had to know everything about that first pregnancy. How she had felt, what she had done, how she had managed, what the miscarriage had been like. Finally she felt the benefit of that sharing. The past slid back to where it should be, less painful than it had ever been.

'I was so shattered when you wouldn't marry me,' he breathed. 'But you were right. Much of it was my ego.'

'I shouldn't have moved out of the apartment so quickly. I was being childish, making a point,' she muttered ruefully. 'I couldn't believe it when you didn't come in search of me. That far, I did trust you even then.'

'I love you so much.' Vito wrapped both arms tightly around her. 'I will never fail you again——'

'You're failing right now.' As he tensed and looked anxiously down into her dancing green eyes, she added softly, running a teasing hand down a long lean thigh, 'I seem to remember something about this guy who gave me fabulous sex...and here I am offering solid gold I'll-never-let-you-go commitment——'

'If you feel like it,' he murmured lazily.

'I do...I do!'

'I'll take them up for their nap.' Fixing a mock-stern expression to her round face, Priya shooed the two giggling little boys up the slope towards the villa. Marco darted back to treat Ashley to a soggy kiss. He was the quiet twin. Carlo, not to be outdone, came tumbling back, dashed a kiss on her cheek and mumbled, 'No nap, Mummy.' He was the pushy one.

Sent back to rejoin Priya, he dragged his plump little legs and threw her a reproachful glance. For a split second he was Vito to the manner born. Susan laughed. 'He's a real little operator, isn't he?'

'I can't believe they're nearly two years old.' Ashley rested back on her lounger and smiled at her sister, thinking how much closer they had become since the twins' birth.

'Time flies when you're enjoying yourself. I wonder what mine will be like.' Susan patted the slight bulge of her once flat stomach. 'I don't care as long as he's healthy.'

'He will be,' Ashley soothed.

'I never thought I would get up the courage...if it hadn't been for the twins——'

'An utterly trouble-free pregnancy,' Ashley reminded her with a grin.

Susan lifted the book that Ashley had been reading, raising a brow at the title. '*Educational Psychology*,' she groaned. 'You have to be out of your mind to want to sign on as a student again.'

'It's something I need to do.'

'I'm amazed Vito agreed.'

Ashley smiled with contentment. 'He understands perfectly.'

Vito strode up with Arnold lagging a few steps in his wake. All burnished brown vitality, he crouched down. 'You look really tired, *cara*.'

'It's all the studying she's trying to do into the bargain,' Susan said disapprovingly.

'It's the heat,' Vito contradicted, springing up.

'You're shameless,' Ashley hissed when they were out of earshot.

Vito followed her upstairs. 'Why should guests change our routine?' He dealt her a wicked grin. 'I can hardly tell your sister that I'm feeling incredibly randy and would she excuse us for a few hours!'

'So I'm just routine now, am I?'

'You're the most gloriously passionate and loved woman alive. And you know it, you shameless hussy,' he reproved, tugging her down on to the bed. 'Let's make the most of the time we have left before your parents arrive.'

'Do you think they'll like it here?' she sighed anxiously.

'Sylvia will love it, but your father...utterly surrounded by foreigners?' Vito gave vent freely to his humour at the prospect.

But Hunt Forrester had changed a great deal. Her parents had ended up seeing a Relate counsellor. The old bullying tactics were no more. Her mother simply wouldn't stand for such treatment now. And through occasional visits and some admittedly awkward discussions Ashley had formed a new relationship with her father. They would never be particularly close, but what they did have was considerably more than she had ever expected to achieve.

'I'm looking forward to seeing Tim.' Her brother was taking a rare break from his medical studies. Vito had been very good to her kid brother, she acknowledged. Whenever they were in London, Tim treated their home as his.

'And while your father is doing his level best to survive his trip abroad, you can continue to find the heat too much in the afternoons,' Vito instructed single-mindedly, running the tip of his tongue seductively along the full line of her lower lip.

She let him claim her mouth in a devouring kiss, felt as always the ripples of excitement begin to build. It never failed. As he shuddered responsively against her, she smiled secretively beneath the rising urgency of his mouth. Some day, when he was in a really good mood, she would ask him who had actually tamed whom.

IT'S FREE! IT'S FUN! ENTER THE

☆ **"Hooray for ☆**
☆ **Hollywood"** ☆

SWEEPSTAKES!

We're giving away prizes to celebrate the screening of four new romance movies on CBS TV this fall! Look for the movies on four Sunday afternoons in October. And be sure to return your Official Entry Coupons to try for a fabulous **vacation in Hollywood!**

☆ If you're the Grand Prize winner we'll fly you and your companion to Los Angeles for a 7-day/6-night vacation you'll never forget!

☆ You'll stay at the luxurious Regent Beverly Wilshire Hotel,* a prime location for celebrity spotting!

☆ You'll have time to visit Universal Studios,* stroll the Hollywood Walk of Fame, check out celebrities' footprints at Mann's Chinese Theater, ride a trolley to see the homes of the stars, and more!

☆ The prize includes a rental car for 7 days and $1,000.00 pocket money!

Someone's going to win this fabulous prize, and it might just be you! Remember, the more times you enter, the better your chances of winning!

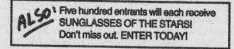

ALSO: Five hundred entrants will each receive SUNGLASSES OF THE STARS! Don't miss out. ENTER TODAY!

The proprietors of the trademark are not associated with this promotion.

CBSIBC

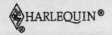 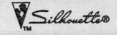

"HOORAY FOR HOLLYWOOD" SWEEPSTAKES

HERE'S HOW THE SWEEPSTAKES WORKS

OFFICIAL RULES — NO PURCHASE NECESSARY

To enter, complete an Official Entry Form or hand print on a 3" x 5" card the words "HOORAY FOR HOLLYWOOD", your name and address and mail your entry in the pre-addressed envelope (if provided) or to: "Hooray for Hollywood" Sweepstakes, P.O. Box 9076, Buffalo, NY 14269-9076 or "Hooray for Hollywood" Sweepstakes, P.O. Box 637, Fort Erie, Ontario L2A 5X3. Entries must be sent via First Class Mail and be received no later than 12/31/94. No liability is assumed for lost, late or misdirected mail.

Winners will be selected in random drawings to be conducted no later than January 31, 1995 from all eligible entries received.

Grand Prize: A 7-day/6-night trip for 2 to Los Angeles, CA including round trip air transportation from commercial airport nearest winner's residence, accommodations at the Regent Beverly Wilshire Hotel, free rental car, and $1,000 spending money. (Approximate prize value which will vary dependent upon winner's residence: $5,400.00 U.S.); 500 Second Prizes: A pair of "Hollywood Star" sunglasses (prize value: $9.95 U.S. each). Winner selection is under the supervision of D.L. Blair, Inc., an independent judging organization, whose decisions are final. Grand Prize travelers must sign and return a release of liability prior to traveling. Trip must be taken by 2/1/96 and is subject to airline schedules and accommodations availability.

Sweepstakes offer is open to residents of the U.S. (except Puerto Rico) and Canada who are 18 years of age or older, except employees and immediate family members of Harlequin Enterprises, Ltd., its affiliates, subsidiaries, and all agencies, entities or persons connected with the use, marketing or conduct of this sweepstakes. All federal, state, provincial, municipal and local laws apply. Offer void wherever prohibited by law. Taxes and/or duties are the sole responsibility of the winners. Any litigation within the province of Quebec respecting the conduct and awarding of prizes may be submitted to the Regie des loteries et courses du Quebec. All prizes will be awarded; winners will be notified by mail. No substitution of prizes are permitted. Odds of winning are dependent upon the number of eligible entries received.

Potential grand prize winner must sign and return an Affidavit of Eligibility within 30 days of notification. In the event of non-compliance within this time period, prize may be awarded to an alternate winner. Prize notification returned as undeliverable may result in the awarding of prize to an alternate winner. By acceptance of their prize, winners consent to use of their names, photographs, or likenesses for purpose of advertising, trade and promotion on behalf of Harlequin Enterprises, Ltd., without further compensation unless prohibited by law. A Canadian winner must correctly answer an arithmetical skill-testing question in order to be awarded the prize.

For a list of winners (available after 2/28/95), send a separate stamped, self-addressed envelope to: Hooray for Hollywood Sweepstakes 3252 Winners, P.O. Box 4200, Blair, NE 68009.

CBSRLS